The Story of Ram

and his friends in the forest

Editor: Mala Dayal

Published 2010 by
Rupa Publications India Pvt. Ltd.
7/16, Ansari Road, Daryaganj,
New Delhi 110 002

Sales Centres:
Allahabad Bengalooru Chandigarh Chennai
Hyderabad Jaipur Kathmandu
Kolkata Mumbai

Printed in India by
Gopsons Papers Ltd.
A-2 & 3, Sector 64
Noida 201 301

The Story of Ram

and his friends in the forest

Pratibha Nath

Illustrated by

Sujasha Dasgupta

Rupa & Co

Come and sit with me and listen to the Ramayan.

The Ramayan is the story of Ram, prince of Ayodhya. It is the story of Ram's life, of his family and the men and monkeys, bears and birds who loved and helped him. The Ramayan is also the story of those who were Ram's enemies and tried to harm him.

It is a very long story, from very old times.

Come, sit with me and listen to the Ramayan.

Long, long ago, on the bank of the river Sarayu, there was a kingdom called Kosala. Its capital was Ayodhya. The king of Kosala was Dasharath.

Dasharath was a good king, just and kind. His people were happy to be ruled by him. But Dasharath had one great sorrow. He had no children. Many years went by. Dasharath kept wishing and praying for a child. Finally he asked for advice from his ministers and priests. They told him that if he performed a certain *yagya* (sacrifice), his prayers would be answered.

At about the same time, the gods in heaven went to Lord Brahma. They said, `O Lord, we are in great trouble. The king of Lanka is a rakshas named Ravan. He has become very proud and cruel. Everyone is afraid of him. The sun does not shine, the wind does not blow and the mighty

ocean itself is stilled when he is around. Ravan is killing both gods and demons. We have heard that he is even thinking of making war on the gods. We beg you to help us. Please rid the earth of Ravan.'

Lord Brahma replied, 'I know Ravan has become very proud and cruel. But, long ago, I myself granted him a boon that no god or demon could defeat him. Because of that boon, Ravan cannot be destroyed by either the gods or other rakshasas. Only a human being can kill him.'

When they heard this, the gods were very upset. Just then Lord Vishnu came by. He was riding his mount, the eagle Garuda. The gods told him about Ravan. Lord Vishnu smiled and said, 'I know Ravan has become very proud and cruel. I also know that he cannot be destroyed by either the gods or other rakshasas. Only a human being can destroy him. But never fear. I shall take on the form of a human being and destroy not only Ravan but the entire race of rakshasas.'

Lord Vishnu kept his promise. He took birth as Ram, the son of King Dasharath. I shall tell you how it happened.

In Ayodhya, Dasharath did what the pundits had suggested. He began to prepare for the *yagya*. It was to be a really grand *yagya*. Hundreds of guests were invited. Hundreds of new buildings were built for the guests to stay in. And a special platform was made for the sacred ceremony. Young cows and bags of gold coins were to be given as gifts to the priests who performed the ceremony. The people of Ayodhya were filled with excitement.

On the day of the great *yagya*, a fire was lit on the platform. Priests began to chant sacred mantras. With a prayer in his heart, King Dasharath poured an offering of ghee on the fire. The flames rose bright and clear. And then a wonderful thing happened. Out of the flames stepped a golden figure, carrying a golden bowl. He told Dasharath, `The gods are pleased with you. They have sent this heavenly *payesh* for your wives. Let them take it and you shall be blessed with children.'

King Dasharath had three queens, Kaushalya, Sumitra and Kaikeyi. He gave the bowl to his queens, starting with the eldest, Kaushalya. He asked each to take half of the *payesh* in the bowl. In the end there was still a little *payesh* left. Dasharath gave it to Sumitra, the second queen.

In time, King Dasharath was blessed with four sons. Ram was born to Kaushalya and Bharat to Kaikeyi. Sumitra had taken the *payesh* twice so she had twins – Lakshman and Shatrughan. The king and his queens were very happy. As for the people of Ayodhya, they were beside themselves with joy. For many days after the birth of the princes, there was merrymaking in Ayodhya.

The four princes grew up. They learnt the holy

books. They also learnt how to shoot with bow and arrow. As time went by, they became skilled in the science of warfare. Right from the beginning, Ram and Lakshman were devoted to one another. Later you shall see how much Ram and Bharat also loved one another.

The years passed. The princes turned fifteen. One day, to the court of King Dasharath, came Sage Vishwamitra. He was wise and learned and everyone respected him. Bowing low before the sage, King Dasharath said, `How can I serve you, Maharaj?'

Sage Vishwamitra was pleased with these words. He said, `O king, as you know, I live in the Dandak forest. I spend my time praying and offering sacrifices to the gods. The king of the rakshasas, Ravan, is bent on disturbing me at my prayers. He has ordered two powerful rakshasas, Mareech and Subahu, to do this. Because of them, I cannot pray in peace. Send Ram with me for a few days to destroy these rakshasas.'

On hearing these words, Dasharath was filled with fear. Ram was so young. How could he fight and destroy two powerful rakshasas? They would surely kill him. Dasharath wanted to say no, but he did not wish to offend the great sage. Besides, Vishwamitra was known to have a bad temper and Dasharath did not want him to get angry. So he agreed.

Ram and Lakshman followed Vishwamitra out of Ayodhya. For three days they walked, till they reached the river Ganga. The sacred waters were alive with swans and cranes and other water birds. Crossing the Ganga, they reached a dense forest. `This is the Dandak forest,' the sage said. `There are many wild animals here –

lions, tigers, elephants and boar. But at one time it was a beautiful place and a lot of people lived here.'

`Where have they all gone?' asked Ram.

`A rakshasi named Tadka and her sons Mareech and Subahu killed a lot of people and the rest ran away,' replied the sage. `Tadka is as strong as a thousand elephants. She kills anyone she sees. Ram, only you can kill her and make this forest a peaceful place once again.'

'I shall do as you command, my lord,' said Ram with folded hands. He held his bow firmly and twanged the bowstring with such force that the forest echoed with the sound. Tadka heard the sound and rushed up, determined to kill Ram and Lakshman. But Ram killed Tadka with a single arrow. Then with a divine weapon given to him by Sage Vishwamitra, Ram killed Subahu. With another weapon, Mareech was hurled far, far away into the sea. With Lakshman's help, Ram destroyed the entire army of rakshasas.

Vishwamitra was very pleased. He embraced the princes and blessed them.

The princes slept peacefully that night. Early the following morning Sage Vishwamitra said to them, `We are going to Mithila, the capital of Videha. Janak, the king of Mithila is performing a *yagya* and we must attend it. At Janak's court you will see a wonderful golden bow. No one has ever been able to string that mighty bow.'

They set off for Mithila. King Janak welcomed them. `Who are these two young men?' he asked Vishwamitra. `They are young and handsome and look as strong as lions. And they carry their weapons like old warriors!'

`They are the sons of King Dasharath,' Vishwamitra replied. `Will you permit them to see the great bow of Shiva that you have in your court?' Long, long ago, Lord Shiva had given his bow to King Janak's forefathers. The bow was kept in an iron box that was mounted on a chariot with eight wheels. It was so heavy that five hundred strong men were needed to pull it.

King Janak had decided that he would give his daughter Sita in marriage to the man who could string Shiva's bow. Many princes had tried to do so, for Sita was the most beautiful maiden in the land. But they had all failed even to lift the mighty bow, let alone bend and string it. Janak looked at Ram and thought to himself, `How can this young lad even lift the bow when so many before him have failed? It is impossible.'

But Ram opened the iron box and lifted out the bow with ease. Not only that. He bent the bow and strung it. Such was Ram's strength that when he drew the string to its fullest extent, the bow broke in two with a sound like thunder. The earth trembled.

Ram had done what nobody else could have even dreamt of doing. You see, Ram was not only the son of King Dasharath. He was Lord Vishnu himself in human form.

King Dasharath was delighted to hear the news of Ram's success. He hurried to Mithila with his queens and many of his nobles. There followed a grand wedding. Ram married Sita and Lakshman married Sita's younger sister Urmila. Bharat and Shatrughan married Sita's cousins Mandavi and Shrutakirti. When the celebrations were over, King Dasharath returned home along with his family and the new brides.

There was great rejoicing in Ayodhya. The city was decorated with flowers and the streets sprinkled with scented water. Music filled the air. At night Ayodhya was lit up with hundreds of lamps. There were sounds of rejoicing in every house.

Ram and Sita were a perfect couple. Sita was always in Ram's thoughts and Ram was always in Sita's heart. For twelve years they lived in great happiness.

And now let me tell you about a time when both Bharat and Shatrughan were away from Ayodhya. They had gone to the kingdom of Kaikeya to visit Bharat's maternal grandfather. Something terrible happened in Ayodhya while these two were away. Wait and I will tell you about it.

King Dasharath was growing old. He decided to step down from the throne. He wanted to make Ram the Crown Prince and let him rule the kingdom. King Dasharath called his ministers and asked their advice. Everyone agreed that Ram should be made Crown Prince. He was wise, brave, kind and just and everyone loved him.

Ram was asked to come to the royal court and was given the news. The people of Ayodhya were delighted when they heard that Ram was to be made Crown Prince. They began to make preparations for the great day.

But one person was not happy to hear that Ram was being made Crown Prince. That person was a hunchback, Manthara. She had been Queen Kaikeyi's maid since Kaikeyi was a young girl. As soon as Manthara heard the news, her heart was filled with evil thoughts. She rushed to Kaikeyi.

But one person was not happy to hear that Ram was being made Crown Prince. That person was a hunchback, Manthara.

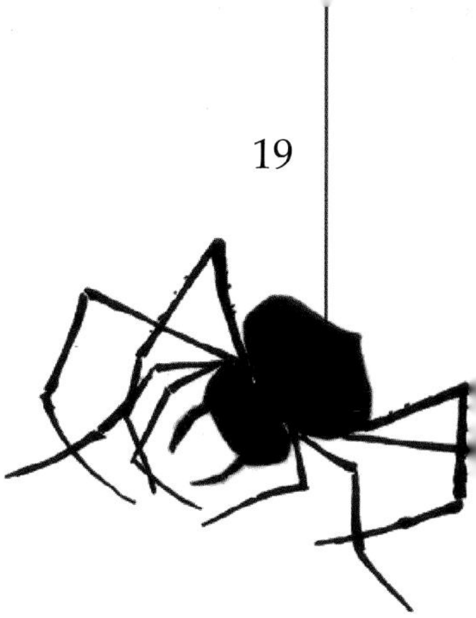

Queen Kaikeyi was in her chamber, full of smiles. Manthara scolded her. `So you are happy to learn that Ram will become Crown Prince tomorrow? Foolish woman, if Ram becomes Crown Prince, his mother Kaushalya will become all-powerful. You will then be no better than her slave. She will give you orders and you will have to obey her. Listen to me: Ram will first become Crown Prince and then king. Your son Bharat will never get a chance to sit on the throne. Why are you smiling? You should be crying!'

Kaikeyi had always loved Ram like her own son. But Manthara's words were like poison. They killed Kaikeyi's love for Ram. `I never thought of this!' she cried. `What should I do? Please help me.' She caught Manthara by the hand.

Manthara told her, `Remember, once the king was wounded in battle and fell unconscious. You carried him to safety and took care of him. He was so grateful that he granted you two boons. Ask the king for those boons now.'

`What shall I ask for?' said Kaikeyi.

Manthara replied at once, `Tell the king to make Bharat Crown Prince instead of Ram. Also, tell him to send Ram away to the forest for fourteen years.... Listen to me. Be firm. Bharat has every right to the throne. He must get it. Ram must not stand in his way.'

What dreadful words! What cruel things to ask for! But Manthara's plan worked. Kaikeyi did as Manthara had told her. She never thought how much pain she would cause King Dasharath, Kaushalya and Ram by asking for those two boons.

When King Dasharath heard Kaikeyi's demands, he was so shocked that he fainted. When he came to his senses, he begged and pleaded with Kaikeyi. `Crops may live without water but I cannot live without Ram,' said King Dasharath. But Kaikeyi would not change her mind. Dasharath's heart was full of sorrow. He had promised Kaikeyi two boons and he was a man of his word. He could not break a promise. It was a matter of honour. To King Dasharath's family, honour was dearer than life itself.

When Ram was given the news that, instead of being made Crown Prince, he was being sent away to the forest for fourteen years, he bowed his head. `If this is my father's wish, I shall obey it,' said Ram. `I would do anything to please my father.'

The very next day, Ram left the palace and all his riches and went to live in the forest like a sadhu. With him went his wife Sita and brother Lakshman. All of Ayodhya wept to see them go. The markets and temples were empty. But the streets were full of people following Ram and begging him to come back. But Ram, Lakshman and Sita never turned back. They spent the next fourteen years in the forest.

Ram left for the forest. For King Dasharath it was the end. He was sunk in sorrow and nobody could comfort him. His grief proved too much for him. A few days later, he passed away. The people of Ayodhya were plunged

in gloom. They had lost both their king and the crown prince. They were now without a ruler.

Swift messengers were sent to Kaikeya to bring Bharat back from his grandfather's place. Bharat was surprised to be called back in such a hurry. On reaching Ayodhya he went straight to the palace. He found it very quiet. The attendants went about their work silently. They would not look at him. They would not speak to him. He looked for his father but his father was not there.

Bharat rushed to Kaikeyi's apartment to find out what had happened. Kaikeyi welcomed him. `Did you have a good journey, my son? How is your grandfather?' she asked.

`He is well and has sent gifts for you,' Bharat replied. 'But why was I called back? Where is my father?'

Kaikeyi replied, `Son, your father lived a long and glorious life. He has now gone to join his ancestors in heaven.'

This was a terrible blow to Bharat. He had loved and respected his father. He asked, `What happened?'

Then Kaikeyi told him what had happened. She said, `Long

ago your father had promised me two boons and I asked for them a few days back. The first boon was that you should be crowned in place of Ram. The second, that Ram should go to the forest to live like a sadhu for fourteen years. All this I did for your sake. You are the king now. I have got the kingdom for you. You should be happy.'

But Bharat was far from happy. He was filled with anger and sorrow. He cried out, `What have you done? I love and respect my brother Ram. Did you really think I would accept the crown that belongs to Ram by right? What a terrible thing you have done! I shall bring Ram back from the forest!'

Leaving Kaikeyi shocked and shaken, Bharat rushed to Kaushalya's apartment. He touched Kaushalya's feet. She blessed him and said, `My son, the crown is waiting for you.'

Bharat fell at her feet. `Mother,' he cried, `you know that I was far away from Ayodhya when all this happened. I had nothing to do with it. How could I do such a thing to my beloved brother Ram? I will never accept the crown. It belongs to Ram and Ram alone.' Kaushalya raised Bharat to his feet and made him sit down. For a long time she talked to him lovingly.

A few days later, the ministers called a meeting. Bharat was invited to attend. Sage Vashisht was the royal priest. He had been adviser to King Dasharath. He said to Bharat, `The king has gone to join his ancestors. Ram and Lakshman are in the forest. The kingdom is without a ruler. We call upon you to accept the crown and rule over the kingdom.'

Bharat's eyes filled with tears. He said, `How can I accept the crown that rightly belongs to my beloved brother? He is the eldest and best among us. I shall go to the

forest to beg Ram to come back. Let us all go and ask Ram to come back to Ayodhya.' Everyone happily agreed.

Preparations began for the great event. Camels, mules, horses and elephants were got ready. A road was prepared, resting places were also made along the way. Food for the journey was collected. When everything was ready, Bharat set out with the army, the three queens, the ministers and many people from the city of Ayodhya.

Bharat went to the forest looking for the brother whom he loved so much. But he did not know where to find Ram. All he knew was that after leaving Ayodhya, Ram, Sita and Lakshman had crossed the mighty river Ganga. Bharat reached the river Ganga and camped on the bank.

On the opposite bank of the Ganga lived Guha, a hunter,

and king of that area. Guha was a good friend of Ram. He saw Bharat's army and suddenly he was afraid Bharat had come to wage war against Ram. Guha immediately climbed into a boat, crossed the Ganga and reached Bharat's camp. He said to Bharat, `You are welcome to this kingdom. But why have you come with an army? I hope you mean no harm to Ram?'

Bharat replied, `I have come to beg Ram to return to Ayodhya and accept the crown.'

Guha was happy to hear this. He said, `Let your army stay here for the night. We shall look after them.'

Early next morning, Guha arranged for boats to take Bharat and his army across the Ganga. Then he guided them to the ashram of Sage Bhardwaj where Ram, Lakshman and Sita had spent a night. The sage asked Bharat, `Why have you come here? You should be in Ayodhya ruling your kingdom. You have not come to do any harm to Ram, have you?'

`How could I ever harm my brother?' Bharat said with tears in his eyes. `I have come to ask him to return to Ayodhya. Please tell me where I can find Ram.'

`Ram is living on Chitrakoot hill,' Sage Bhardwaj replied. `Spend the night in my ashram. Tomorrow I shall show you the way to Ram's hut on Chitrakoot hill.'

Next morning they took the path shown by the sage. After some time, in the distance, they saw a dense forest. Rising above the forest was Chitrakoot hill. Blue smoke rose from a hut on the hill. Bharat told the others to stay back. Only he, Sage Vashisht and the royal charioteer went forward to meet Ram.

It was Sage Bhardwaj who had told Ram about Chitrakoot hill. 'You will find it a very pleasant place to stay in,' he had said. And he was right. Chitrakoot hill stood on the bank of a river. There

were many streams running down the hill, gushing with clear, sweet water. There were roots and fruits enough to eat.

Sita, in particular, was very happy at Chitrakoot. The forest had wild flowers of different colours. Champa flowers shone white and gold among dark green leaves. Palash trees stood laden with crimson blooms. Flowering creepers hung from trees like garlands. The forest paths were shaded by bamboos, making them green and cool and beautiful. Koels and doves sang as they flitted from tree to tree. Peacocks danced and monkeys chattered. Deer peeped out from behind the trees and bushes. Elephants, lions and wild boar roamed the forest.

Under a fine, spreading banyan tree Lakshman had built a strong hut of bamboo, leaves and grass. All three lived happily in the hut. They performed their daily worship and enjoyed the peace and beauty of the forest. They almost forgot that they were in exile.

Then one day, the peace of the forest was disturbed. Ram and Lakshman saw a cloud of dust in the distance. `What is that rumbling sound, Lakshman?' asked Ram.

Lakshman climbed a tall tree and looked around. He saw Bharat's army with its horses and elephants, chariots and soldiers. `O my brother, it is Bharat,' said Lakshman. `He has come with his army. I can see his flag fluttering in the breeze. Send Sita into the hut. Get your bow and arrows ready.'

`Bharat is not coming to kill us,' said Ram calmly. `He is coming to ask me to come back to Ayodhya and accept the crown.'

Bharat reached Chitrakoot. He climbed up a sal tree and saw the smoke from Ram's hut. Shouting, `Ram is here!' Bharat raced up the hill and entered the hut. Ram was seated before the sacred fire. He was dressed, not like a prince, but like a sadhu. He wore deerskin and the bark of trees. But he looked majestic and strong as a lion. After all, he was none other than Lord Vishnu himself!

Bharat fell at Ram's feet. So great was Bharat's love for Ram and his sorrow over what had happened that he began to cry.

Ram lifted up Bharat and embraced him. On hearing that King Dasharath had died, Ram was plunged in grief. Bharat said, 'Our father died of grief at parting from you. Undo the great wrong that has been done. I beg you, come back to Ayodhya and accept the crown.'

Ram replied, 'Do not feel sad over what has happened. And do not blame your mother. We must obey our father's wishes. It is your duty to obey our father and rule over the kingdom. And it is my duty to obey him and live in the forest for fourteen years.'

Again and again Bharat begged Ram to come back. But Ram was firm. In the end Bharat said to Ram, 'Give me your sandals. I shall place them on the throne to show that you are the real ruler. I shall rule in your name till you come back.'

Bharat took Ram's sandals and returned to Ayodhya. He placed the sandals on the throne and announced,

'The kingdom is not mine. It is Ram's. I will look after the kingdom till Ram returns. And I shall live, not in a palace in Ayodhya but in a village.'

The story of Ram will live for ever. The names of Lakshman and Bharat will live for ever too. People will never forget these two wonderful brothers of Ram. Lakshman became a sadhu to be with Ram in the forest. And Bharat refused the crown because it belonged to Ram by right.

After Bharat left, Ram did not wish to live at Chitrakoot. So he, Sita and Lakshman left Chitrakoot. For many years they wandered about the forest, spending their time in different ashrams. Everywhere the rishis welcomed them. Once they lived in the ashram of Sage Agastya who was known for his wisdom and piety. By then the period of exile was almost over. Sage Agastya advised Ram to spend the rest of the fourteen years at Panchvati, on the bank of the river Godavari. Following the sage's advice, Ram, Lakshman and Sita set off for Panchvati.

Panchvati proved to be beautiful indeed. Ram and Lakshman found the ideal place to build a hut. It was a clearing in the forest, surrounded by *kadamb* trees. Each tree bore a crown of fresh green leaves. A small stream flowed close by, with blue lotuses floating on it. Further away there were mountains, with herds of deer roaming on the grassy slopes. Elephants came to bathe in the stream and peacocks danced in the sunlight.

Sita loved Panchvati. Lakshman built a comfortable hut in the clearing. Ram, Sita and Lakshman lived there happily.

The days at Panchvati passed peacefully. Sita spent her time gathering flowers and stringing them. She made friends with the birds, the deer and the peacocks. She offered them food and they came near and ate from her hand. The hills and woods grew lovelier every day and the birds and beasts welcomed Ram, Sita and Lakshman.

Days turned into nights and nights turned into days again. Time flew. Then one day, there came to Panchvati a rakshasi named Srupnakha.

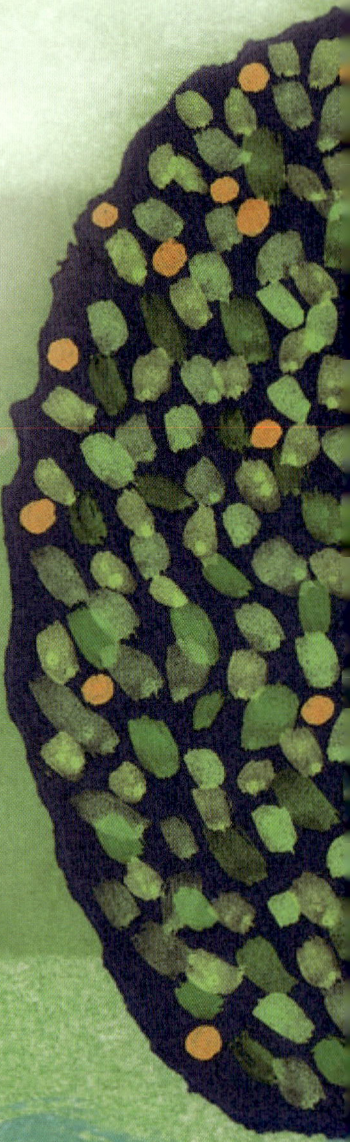

Srupnakha was the sister of Ravan, the king of Lanka. She also lived in the Dandak forest, at a place called Janasthan, close to Panchvati. Many rakshasas lived at Janasthan. Among them were two other brothers of Srupnakha. Their names were Khar and Dooshan.

One morning, when Ram and Lakshman were sitting near their hut, Srupnakha saw them. Ram was very handsome and Srupnakha fell in love with him. She went up to him and said, `How handsome you are! Be my husband and live with me. Do not worry about your wife Sita. I will eat her up and you will be rid of her. Then you and I can enjoy the beauty of the Dandak forest.'

Ram laughed. He said gently, `I am already married. I dearly love my wife Sita. But my younger brother Lakshman is not married. He is strong, brave and handsome. Why not ask him to be your husband?'

Srupnakha went to Lakshman and asked him to marry her. Lakshman knew that Ram was joking. He carried the joke further. `You should

become the second wife of my brother,' said Lakshman. 'He has everything. I am only his slave.'

Srupnakha did not realise that the brothers were joking. She saw Sita sitting close to Ram and flew into a temper. She sprang at Sita, wanting to catch her and eat her up. Ram saved Sita just in time and said to Lakshman, `This has gone too far. Teach this creature a lesson.' At this, Lakshman drew his sword and cut off Srupnakha's nose.

Bleeding and screaming with pain, Srupnakha ran to Khar. `Who dared do this to you?' he roared in anger. She told him the whole story. Khar swore revenge. He sent fourteen mighty rakshasas to kill Ram and Lakshman. But Ram killed the fourteen rakshasas with fourteen arrows. Next, Khar sent his army along with Dooshan to kill Ram and Lakshman. But Ram killed all of them too. Finally, Khar came himself, armed with a mace. But one arrow from Ram's bow and Khar lay dead on the ground.

At last the Dandak forest was rid of all the rakshasas. The sages living there were very happy. But for Ram, Lakshman and Sita serious trouble was in store. The rakshasas had become their bitter enemies.

When Khar and Dooshan were killed by Ram, Srupnakha rushed to Lanka. She went to Ravan's durbar and screamed, `You are seated here in all your glory, with no idea of what is happening elsewhere! Do you know that Janasthan has been destroyed? Fourteen thousand rakshasas living there have been killed, along with your brothers Khar and Dooshan. All this was done by Ram alone. And see what Ram and Lakshman have done to me!'

Ravan was shocked. `Who is this Ram?' he roared.

`Ram is the son of Dasharath who was king of Ayodhya,' replied Srupnakha. `He is living in the forest and is brave and

strong. His brother Lakshman is also living in the forest. He is also brave and strong and is devoted to Ram. Ram has a beautiful wife named Sita. I have never seen a woman as beautiful as her. She would be the ideal wife for you. Go and capture her. Make her your wife. That way Ram will be disgraced. And you will pay him back for killing all the rakshasas and for wounding your sister.'

Srupnakha was very cunning. She wanted Ram to be disgraced. She also knew that Ram loved Sita very much. If he lost Sita, he would be heartbroken. Then it would be easy to defeat him. That is why Srupnakha thought of this plan.

When Ravan heard Srupnakha praise the beauty of Sita, he decided to carry Sita away and make her his wife. Ravan went to see the rakshas Mareech. He told Mareech the whole story. `I want to punish Ram by carrying off his wife Sita,' said Ravan. `For that I need your help. Turn yourself into a golden deer with silver spots. Make yourself more beautiful than any other animal on earth. Then go to the Dandak forest. I want you to graze in front of Ram's hut, within sight of Ram and Sita. When Sita sees the deer, she will beg Ram to catch it, so she can keep it as a pet. Ram will go after the deer. You must lure both Ram and Lakshman away from the hut. When they have left, Sita will be alone. There will be nobody to protect her. That is the time when I shall carry her away.'

When Mareech heard Ravan's wicked plan, he was horrified. He said, `This deed will surely bring disaster upon you! You do not know Ram's strength. I beg of you, stop thinking of making Sita your wife. She will turn you into a heap of ashes with her anger!' But Ravan did not listen to Mareech's advice. In the end, Mareech had to agree to Ravan's plan. After all, Ravan was his king.

One morning, Sita was gathering flowers when she saw the most beautiful deer. It was very different from the deer that roamed about the forest. Its body was golden in colour and covered with shiny silver spots. Its horns were set with jewels in all the colours of the rainbow. They sparkled when the deer moved its head.

The deer wandered about in front of the hut. Sometimes it nibbled the soft grass. Sometimes it wandered about before the banana trees in front of the hut. Sometimes it would rush off as if in a hurry. At other times it would stand still and gaze at Sita with a soft, gentle look in its eyes.

The deer cast a spell on Sita. She kept looking at it as she gathered flowers. She had never before seen anything so beautiful. She

called Ram and Lakshman. They came out of the hut and stood for a long time, staring at the deer.

It was Lakshman who spoke first. 'I am sure this is not a deer at all. It is a rakshas in disguise. This is a work of magic. I have never heard of a deer with a golden skin, covered with silver spots and with horns set with jewels. This is some trick.'

Ram agreed. He turned to Sita. 'This is not a real deer. It is a trick played by a rakshas. They know magic and can take on any form they like.'

But Sita was bent on having the deer. 'You must capture it and bring it to me,' she said to Ram. 'You must. I will not know any peace unless I have it for a pet.'

Ram loved Sita very much. If she wanted anything, he always tried to get it for

her. But the deer was a different matter. Ram wanted to keep away from it. He said to Sita gently, 'Why do you want that deer? There are so many other animals and birds in the forest. There are elephants that come to bathe in the Godavari. There are monkeys and squirrels and beautiful birds like the *saras* and *nilkanth*. You love them and they love you. They come to your door and eat from your hands. Forget about this deer. There is something strange about it.'

But Sita would not listen. She went on asking Ram to go after the deer and capture it. In the end Ram gave in. He picked up his bow and arrows and left. As he was leaving, he told Lakshman, 'Look after Sita. Stay here. Do not leave Sita alone.'

Ram went near the deer. When he got near it, the deer moved away a short distance. Then it stood still and nibbled some grass. This happened again and again. The deer would show itself to Ram and then move away. In this way, the deer led Ram far away from the hut, deep into the forest. Finally, tired of the chase,

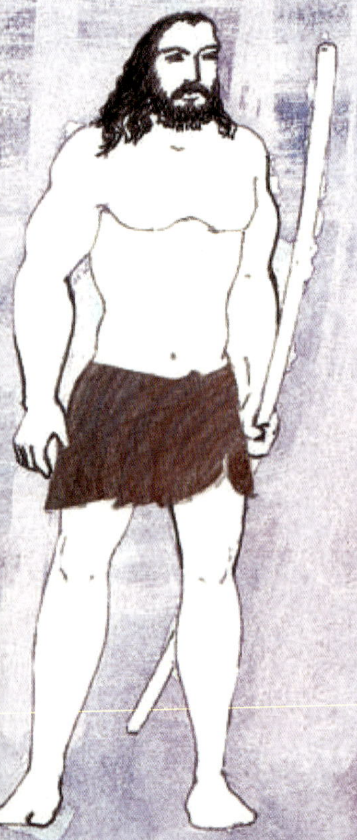

Ram shot the deer with an arrow. As the deer fell to the ground, it changed into the rakshas Mareech. His body was like a mountain and he had enormous teeth. Just before he died, the rakshas cried out, `O Sita! O Lakshman!' His voice sounded just like Ram's.

Back in the hut, Sita heard the cry which sounded just like Ram's. She thought Ram had been hurt. She told Lakshman to go quickly and help Ram. Lakshman was certain that Ram had not

come to any harm because he was so powerful. But Sita insisted that he should go because she felt Ram needed help.

Lakshman refused to obey her because he was worried about her safety. He told Sita, `That beautiful golden deer with silver spots and that cry "O Sita, O Lakshman" are a clever plot against us. It was not Ram's voice that we heard. With their magical powers rakshasas can do anything. I will not leave you alone.'

When Lakshman refused to obey her, Sita became angry. She said, `You have no love for your brother.' Finally Lakshman had to obey her. He said, `Very well, I shall do as you say. But for your protection I shall draw a magic circle around the hut. Whatever happens, you must not cross this circle. You will be safe as long as you stay within the circle. May the gods protect you!' And, with the point of an arrow, Lakshman drew a circle on the ground all around the hut. This is known as the `Lakshman Rekha'. He then set off in the direction that Ram had taken.

All this while Ravan had been hiding among the trees surrounding the hut. When he saw Lakshman leave, Ravan took on the form of a sadhu. He wore saffron robes and sandals on his feet. His hair was tied in a knot on top of his head. He carried a staff in one hand, a rosary in the other and he was chanting vedic mantras. But he had evil in his heart as he slowly approached the hut.

Ravan stood outside the charmed circle, called out a

blessing and asked for alms.

Sita went inside the hut and returned with some food. She offered the food to Ravan from within the circle.

'Bring it to me here, daughter,' said the sadhu, standing where he was.

`I must not step outside this circle,' said Sita.

`Then I shall go away without the alms. May the Lord forgive you!' With these words, the sadhu began to walk away.

Sita felt ashamed at having turned away a hungry sadhu. `Maharaj! Maharaj!' she called after him. `Forgive me. Please come back.' In her eagerness to call the sadhu back and give him alms, she forgot about Lakshman's warning and stepped outside the magic circle.

The moment she stepped outside the magic circle, the sadhu took the form of Ravan. He pounced on Sita and dragged her into the forest. He held her firmly and told her who he really was. He described the greatness of his family, his power and wealth. `I am Ravan, the great rakshas king of Lanka,' said Ravan. `Rivers stop flowing, leaves do not dance on trees, the wind dare not blow where I go. Even the sun is frightened of me. Give up that worthless husband of yours. Come to Lanka and be my queen.'

Her eyes red with anger, Sita cried, `I am devoted to Ram. He is like a lion, while you are just a jackal. He is like a majestic elephant, you a miserable cat. If you value your life, put me down and leave this place at once.' Ravan was furious. Catching Sita by the hair, he lifted her up and forced her into his flying chariot which could go anywhere. The chariot rose into the sky.

It was a terrible moment. Terrible because Ravan was committing a great sin and the entire forest was witness to it. A deathlike silence fell over the forest. The trees held their breath, the flowers closed their petals in fright. Ravan's face had become red with anger and birds and beasts fled from his path. Even the river Godavari flowed softly, scared of Ravan' s angry looks.

As the chariot rose into the air, Sita sobbed aloud. She cried out to Ram and Lakshman to save her. They were far away in the forest and did not hear her. But someone else did.

It was the old bird Jatayu, king of the vultures and a close friend of King Dasharath.

Jatayu was dozing on the top of a tree. He woke up when he heard Sita's cries for help. Jatayu was very big and had a sharp beak. He told Ravan, `O king, listen to me. I am Jatayu, king of the vultures. Do not do this shameful thing. If you have a complaint against Ram, fight him face to face. Why are you carrying off his wife Sita? Let her go. I will not let you take her away as long as I am alive.'

Ravan became even angrier at Jatayu's words. He shot arrow after arrow at the great bird. Jatayu attacked the chariot with his sharp beak and claws. So fierce was the

attack that Ravan's chariot was smashed to bits. Ravan fell to the ground, but he still held Sita in his grip.

Ravan noticed that old Jatayu was getting tired. He rose into the air once again with Sita. Jatayu attacked Ravan and tore off his arms. But Ravan had twenty arms. No sooner was one torn off than another grew in its place. Finally Ravan drew his sword and cut off Jatayu's wings. The wingless bird fell to the ground, unable to move. He was totally helpless, with hardly a breath left in his body.

Sita ran to Jatayu. She wept to see him so badly hurt. `You have given your life for me!' she cried.

Ravan again rushed towards Sita to carry her away. To escape Ravan, Sita ran through the forest and clung to the trees. `O my Ram, where are you?' she cried. But Ravan caught her and rose with her into the air.

Ravan carried Sita through the sky. They went over rivers and lakes, forests and mountains. Birds and beasts ran behind Sita's shadow on the ground as if to give her courage and tell her not to be afraid. Even the sun turned pale as Sita was being carried away by Ravan.

Sita looked around for someone who could help her, but saw no one. As they were flying over a mountain, Sita noticed five very big monkeys sitting on its peak. Sita took off her necklaces and bangles, tied them in a piece of silk torn from her sari and threw the bundle among the monkeys. She did so hoping that

they would tell Ram the direction in which she had been taken. Ravan did not see Sita throw the bundle.

Ravan reached the beautiful city of Lanka and went straight to his palace. He took Sita to the inner apartments and ordered some rakshasis to guard her. `Give her whatever she asks for – gold, jewels, clothes,' Ravan told the rakshasis. `And honour her as you would honour me.'

In the days that followed, Ravan showed Sita his enormous wealth. His palace had huge buildings. Jewels glittered and shone from all sides. He showed Sita beautiful lotus pools surrounded by flowering trees. He told her that no king in the world was as powerful as him. He asked Sita to marry him.

But Sita put a blade of grass between herself and Ravan and said angrily, `Ram is like a god to me. He will order the ocean to dry up in order to reach here. He will kill you and take me back.'

Ravan was furious. He said, `I give you twelve months. If by that time you do not agree to marry me, you shall die.'

Ravan then turned to the rakshasis. `Take Sita to the Ashok Vatika and guard her well.'

The rakshasis took Sita to the Ashok grove. The grove was full of flowering creepers and fruit trees. Birds sang and flitted among the trees. But Sita found no pleasure in all this. She thought only of Ram.

Let us now go back to the hut at Panchvati. What was happening there all this while? As you saw, Ram had left the hut because Sita went on insisting that he should go after the deer and capture it. Ram followed the golden deer through the forest. On and on they went, in and out among the trees. Ram gave chase till, finally, he got tired. With a single arrow, Ram killed the golden deer. As the deer fell to the ground, it changed into the rakshas Mareech. It cried, 'O Sita! O Lakshman!' in a voice just like Ram's.

Ram was filled with worry for Sita. Looking at the mountain-like rakshas lying on the ground, he thought, 'Lakshman was right. This *was* a trick to get me away from the hut. Sita is in great danger!'

Ram was hurrying back to the hut when he met Lakshman coming to meet him. 'Why did you leave Sita alone?' cried Ram. Lakshman told him the whole story, with tears in his eyes. The two brothers rushed back to the hut.

Just as they had feared, they found the hut empty. There were some champa flowers scattered on the ground. 'These are the flowers I gave her this morning,' cried Ram. 'They must have fallen from her hair. O Sita, where are you?'

Calling out to Sita again and again, Ram ran through the forest like one gone mad. Lakshman went with him, trying to comfort him. He said, 'My brother, do not grieve. Sita must be somewhere around.'

But Ram was beside himself with grief. He

begged the creepers and the trees to tell him where Sita was. He asked the animals and birds, fish and bees to tell him where Sita had gone. Ram searched all over the forest but found no trace of Sita.

At long last the brothers came upon Jatayu, big as a mountain, lying on the ground. Jatayu had only a few moments left to live. But, to the very end, he was a loyal friend. He told Ram, 'Sita has been carried away by Ravan. He has taken her towards the south. I tried to fight Ravan but he cut off my wings. Attack his kingdom, kill Ravan and you will be able to get back Sita.' With these words Jatayu closed his eyes and died.

'This mighty bird died for me,' said Ram sadly. Both Ram and Lakshman were very sad to lose a loyal friend. But the search for Sita had to go on. So they set off in the direction that Jatayu had pointed out.

Suddenly, a sound like thunder shook the forest. Ram and Lakshman looked around and saw a huge, ugly monster who had neither head nor neck. His mouth was on his belly. He had two very long arms. Without moving from his place, he would stretch out his arms, catch bears, flocks of birds and herds of deer and eat them.

When the rakshas saw Ram and Lakshman, he stretched out his arms and caught them. He was about to swallow them when the princes cut off his arms. The rakshas was now quite helpless. He told the princes, 'Long ago I was strong and handsome. But I was very proud. One day, a sage got angry with me. He cursed me. I was to live in this form till Ram cut off my arms and killed me.'

At the rakshas's request, Ram and Lakshman killed and cremated him. From the fire arose a handsome man. He told Ram and Lakshman, `You will certainly get Sita back. Go to Rishyamook hill near Lake Pampa. There you will find Sugreev. He has been driven out of his kingdom Kishkinda by his brother Bali. He lives in constant fear. Make friends with him and ask him to send his followers to forests, mountains and caves to look for your wife Sita.'

Ram said to Lakshman, `I am sure Sugreev will be able to help me find Sita. Let us go towards Rishyamook hill.'

The journey took many days. At long last Ram and Lakshman reached Lake Pampa. The lake was deep and beautiful. On the banks were flowering trees of many kinds – *bakul, kadamb,* and flame of the forest. There were jackfruit and mango trees as well. Their flowers filled the air with sweet fragrance. It was the spring season and a gentle breeze scattered flowers all over the ground. Bees buzzed noisily, koels sang happy songs and peacocks danced. Blue and pink lotus flowers floated on the surface of the lake. Swans and cranes, geese and other water birds flocked to the lake and fish leapt in the clear water. Lake Pampa was indeed a very beautiful place.

Ram looked at the beauty around him. How he wished Sita were there to enjoy it with him! He remembered how much Sita loved flowers. He also remembered how the call of the geese had amused Sita. She always laughed when she heard

it. These memories filled Ram with sorrow. For a long time he stood in silence. Then, pulling himself together, he said to Lakshman, 'There, in the distance, stands Rishyamook hill where Sugreev is said to live. Let us go and meet him.'

Who was Sugreev, on whom Ram had pinned his hopes?

Sugreev was a monkey prince. He had an elder brother named Bali. Bali had driven Sugreev out of his kingdom Kishkinda. Bali had even taken away Sugreev's wife. Homeless and heartbroken, Sugreev had taken shelter in a cave on Rishyamook hill. He lived in the cave with a few monkey friends. Sugreev was afraid Bali would attack him again. So he did not trust any stranger who came to Rishyamook hill.

One day, when Sugreev was sitting in the cave with his friends, he saw Ram and Lakshman coming towards the hill. They seemed to be looking for someone. Sugreev was filled with fear. He said to Hanuman, his adviser, `Go and find out who these strangers are and why they have come here.'

Hanuman took the form of a brahmin and went to meet the strangers. He was afraid they might turn out to be enemies. But as soon as he met them, his fears melted away. He told them he was Hanuman, son of the wind god and Sugreev's adviser. He told them that he could take any form he wanted and go wherever he wished.

Hanuman's speech was so polite and beautiful that Ram felt he could be trusted completely. The three of them stood on the hillside and talked as if they had known each other for a long time. Hanuman related the story of Sugreev and how he had lost both his kingdom and his wife to Bali. Hanuman said, `Sugreev is looking for someone who will defeat Bali and restore to him (Sugreev) his kingdom and his wife.'

Ram and Lakshman told Hanuman about themselves and how they were looking for Sita. Ram said, `We have come here to seek Sugreev's help in bringing Sita back.' It was clear that Ram and Sugreev had a similar problem. Sugreev needed help to defeat Bali and get back his kingdom and his wife. Ram needed help to find Sita and free her from the clutches of Ravan. Ram and Sugreev could be of great help to one another.

All three went to Sugreev. Hanuman went ahead and told Sugreev about Ram and Lakshman. `The two brothers are truly worthy of your friendship,' he told Sugreev. `In fact, they will be a great help to you if you make friends with them.'

Sugreev, Ram and Lakshman talked for a long time. There was perfect agreement among them. Hanuman then lit a fire. Ram and Sugreev walked around it as a mark of everlasting friendship.

Then Sugreev told Ram, `Let me tell you about something that happened a few days ago. My friends and I were sitting on top

of this hill, as we often do. Suddenly we saw something in the sky. It was a rakshas, dark as a rain cloud and just as big. With his left arm he held a beautiful woman who glowed like a streak of lightning. She was struggling and crying out, "O Ram! O Lakshman!" From what you have told me, it must have been your wife whom the rakshas was carrying away. When she saw me and my friends, she threw in our midst a small bundle tied in yellow silk. The woman had taken off some of her ornaments, hurriedly

tied them in a piece of silk torn from her sari and dropped the bundle in our midst. Perhaps she hoped that you would get to know of it. I have kept the bundle safely. I will bring it to you. See if it belongs to Sita.'

Sugreev brought a small bundle tied in yellow silk and placed it before Ram. Ram recognised the silk. It was from Sita's favourite sari. With trembling hands Ram picked up the jewels, one by one. Tears poured down his face and he grew as pale as the

sun in winter. 'Sita!' he cried out and fell down in a faint. When he recovered, he said to Lakshman, 'I am overcome with grief at the sight of these jewels. My eyes are blinded with tears. Tell me, do you recognise these necklaces and bangles? Do they belong to Sita?'

Lakshman was in tears too. He said, 'I cannot recognise her necklaces and bangles because I never raised my eyes to her face or hands. But these anklets I recognise because every morning I touched her feet to seek her blessings.'

Sugreev was deeply touched by Ram's love for Sita. He missed his wife very much and understood Ram's grief. He promised to help Ram find Sita. And Ram, in turn, promised to help Sugreev get back his wife and his kingdom.

Ram and Sugreev had promised to help one another. But Sugreev was not sure if Bali could be defeated. Bali was very strong. His body was like iron. Sugreev began to

wonder if Ram would be able to kill Bali.

One day, they were sitting near a grove of sal trees. Sugreev said, `Look at those trees, so straight and tall. Look at their thick branches. My brother Bali can pull out a sal tree by its roots and shake it till all the leaves fall off.'

Ram understood that Sugreev wanted to test his strength. He lifted his bow, fitted it with an arrow and shot the arrow at the sal trees. The arrow flew through the air and pierced not one but seven sal trees that stood in a row. Sugreev was delighted. He was now sure that Ram could pierce the iron frame of Bali. So eager was he to get back his kingdom and his wife that he said excitedly, `Let us go to Kishkinda at once.'

They all set off for Kishkinda. When they reached there, Ram and Lakshman hid behind some trees. Sugreev went ahead. He stood at the gate of the palace and challenged Bali to a fight.

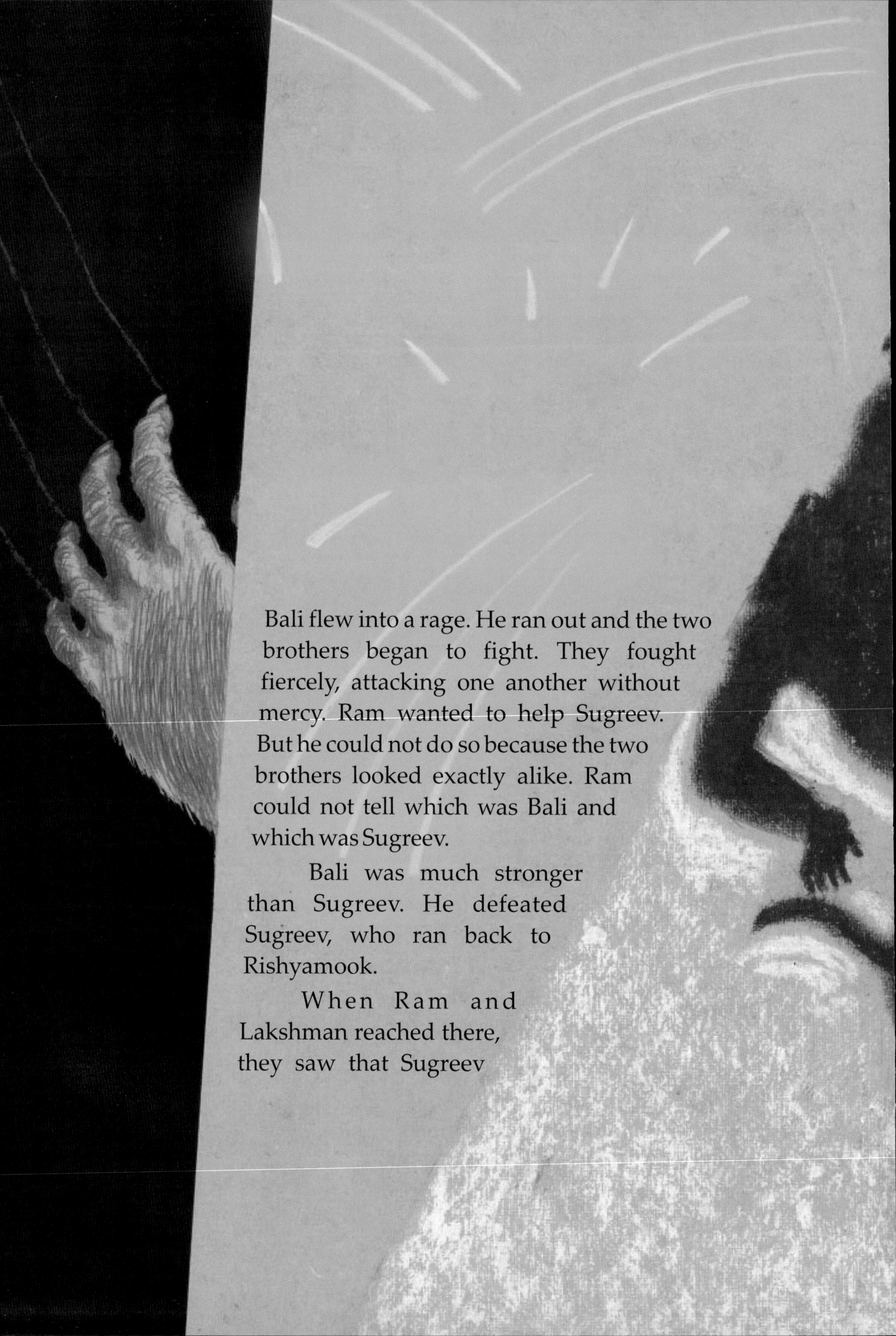

Bali flew into a rage. He ran out and the two brothers began to fight. They fought fiercely, attacking one another without mercy. Ram wanted to help Sugreev. But he could not do so because the two brothers looked exactly alike. Ram could not tell which was Bali and which was Sugreev.

Bali was much stronger than Sugreev. He defeated Sugreev, who ran back to Rishyamook.

When Ram and Lakshman reached there, they saw that Sugreev

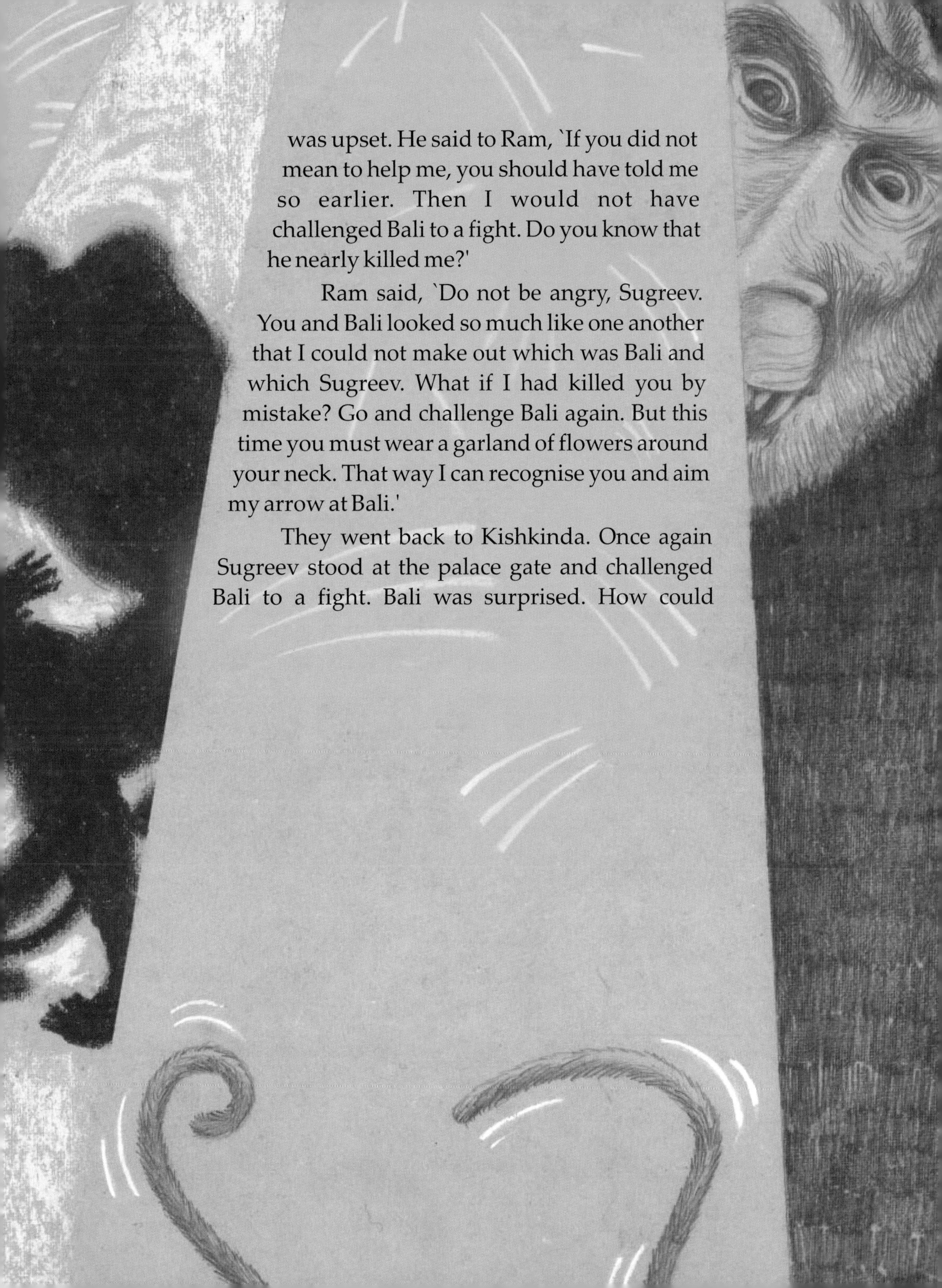

was upset. He said to Ram, 'If you did not mean to help me, you should have told me so earlier. Then I would not have challenged Bali to a fight. Do you know that he nearly killed me?'

Ram said, 'Do not be angry, Sugreev. You and Bali looked so much like one another that I could not make out which was Bali and which Sugreev. What if I had killed you by mistake? Go and challenge Bali again. But this time you must wear a garland of flowers around your neck. That way I can recognise you and aim my arrow at Bali.'

They went back to Kishkinda. Once again Sugreev stood at the palace gate and challenged Bali to a fight. Bali was surprised. How could

Sugreev come back so soon and challenge him to another fight? Had Sugreev not been beaten? In fact, he had been beaten so badly that he had to run for his life.

Bali came out to fight. Sugreev was sure that Ram would help him this time. For a long time the two brothers fought fiercely. Finally Bali's greater strength began to tell. Ram saw that Sugreev would not be able to keep up the fight much longer. Ram took careful aim and shot an arrow that pierced Bali's chest. Bali crashed to the ground.

As he lay dying, Bali said to Ram, `Why did you kill me when I was fighting someone else? That was very wrong.'

Ram replied, `You do not deserve to live. You have taken your brother's wife and that is a great sin. You deserve to die. That is why I have killed you.'

Bali realised that he had done wrong. He said to Sugreev, `What a pity we became enemies! We could have been friends and ruled over our kingdom together. It is too late now. I am dying. The kingdom is yours. I leave my son Angad in your care. Look after him.' Bali could say no more. He blessed his brother and died.

Ram had fulfilled his promise to Sugreev. He had killed Bali. With Bali's death, Sugreev once again became king of Kishkinda. He got back his wife, his kingdom and all his treasure. He began to enjoy life in the company of his friends. Sugreev forgot all about his promise to Ram. Months passed and nothing was done to find Sita.

While Sugreev enjoyed himself in Kishkinda, Ram and Lakshman lived in a cave nearby. Around them were trees and bushes covered with flowering creepers. Springs sparkled and danced. But Ram and Lakshman were lonely and very sad. There was a reason for their sadness. The rainy season had set in. Clouds gathered in the sky, the sound of thunder could be heard and

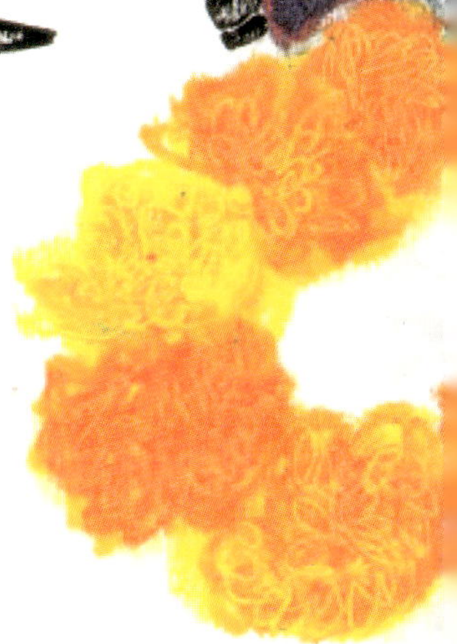

lightning flashed. Soon it began to rain day and night. Forest paths became rushing rivers. Ram and Lakshman could not even walk on them and go looking for Sita.

At last the rains were over. The sky became blue again. Joy filled the forest. Ram said to Lakshman, `All the world is full of joy. But Sita must be very unhappy. She is held captive by rakshasas. If only Sugreev would remember his promise and help me find Sita. Go to Kishkinda and remind him of his promise to me.'

Sugreev may have forgotten his promise to Ram, but Hanuman remembered it. One day he said to Sugreev, `Ram has fulfilled his promise to you. But you had also made a promise to him and that remains unfulfilled. The rainy season is over. Let us not delay the search for Sita any more.'

Sugreev took Hanuman's advice. Calling his generals he said, `We must search for Sita everywhere. Order the powerful monkeys and bears from the four corners of the land to come here at once.'

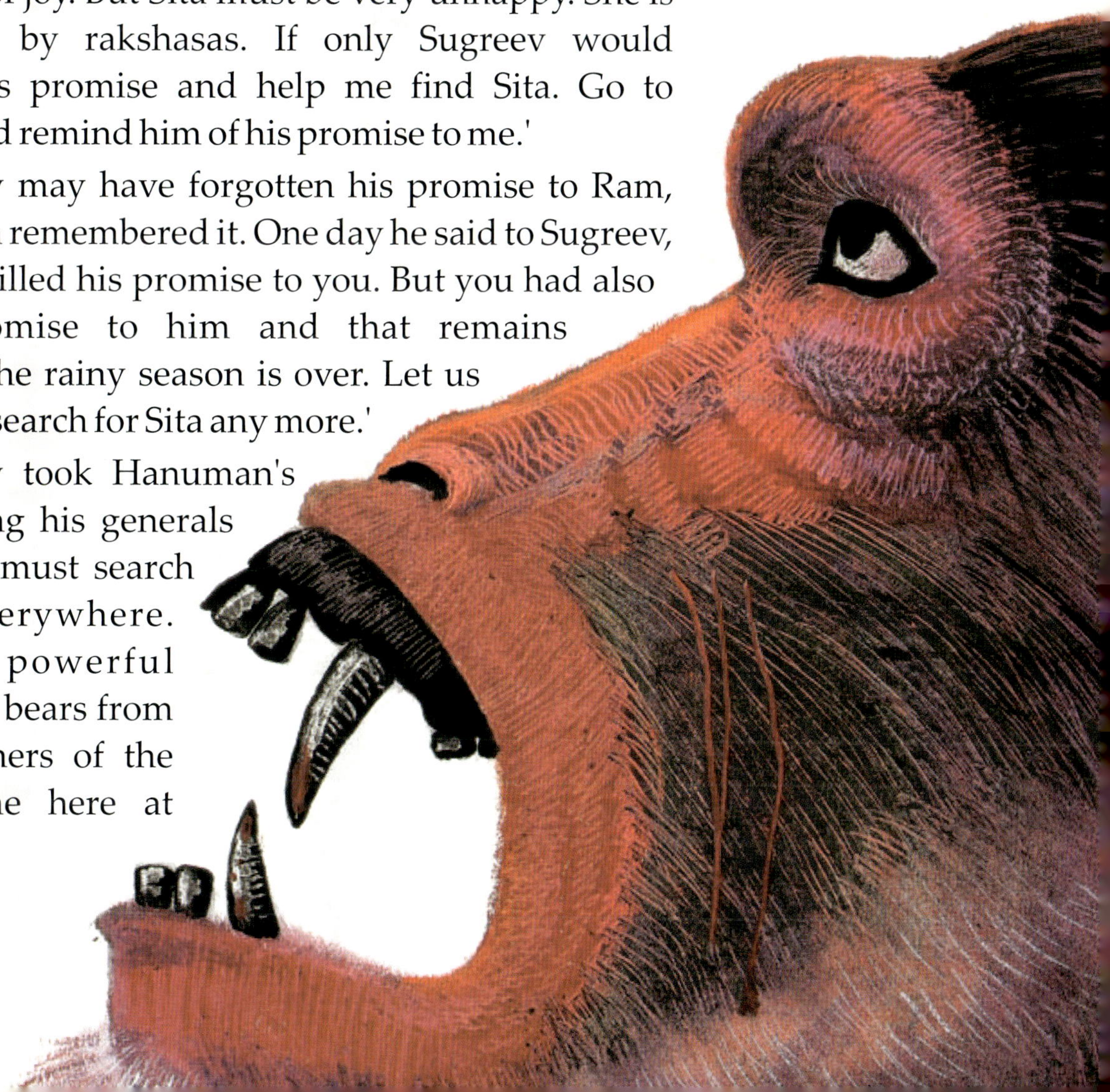

The generals hurried to obey the king's orders. Just then Lakshman arrived at the gates of Kishkinda. Lakshman was very angry with Sugreev. The anger showed on his face. He twanged the string of his mighty bow and the great sound filled all of Kishkinda with fear.

Sugreev now came out to meet Lakshman. With folded hands he said, `Forgive me. It is with Ram's help that I am king today. How can I ever forget that? The search for Sita will begin very soon.'

Sugreev and Lakshman then went to Ram. Soon huge armies of mighty monkeys and bears arrived with their leaders. They came from distant forests and mountains. They had crossed hills, valleys and rivers. The dust they raised darkened the sky. There were millions of monkeys and bears, of different sizes and colours. They spread as far as the eye could see. It was an impressive sight.

Proudly pointing to the mighty monkey and bear armies, Sugreev said, `They are famous for their strength. They can find their way through the densest of forests. They will fight with their sharp teeth and nails, kill Ravan and bring Sita back to you.'

At last Ram and Sugreev were working together. Their friendship had borne fruit and the search for Sita had begun. Sugreev gave strict orders to his commanders to take divisions of the army to the four corners of the earth and search for Sita. He said, `Go to the mountains, forests and rivers, to caves, the countryside and cities and look for Sita. Return within one month with news of Sita. Anyone who fails to carry out these orders will be punished with death.'

Within a day divisions of the army had marched off in three different directions. But Sugreev had the greatest hopes of Hanuman who was the son of Vayu, the wind god. Hanuman had great strength, courage and wisdom. He could move with the speed of the wind. He could also leap across oceans. Sugreev took Hanuman aside and said, `I am relying on you to discover where Sita is.'

Ram also felt that Hanuman would be successful. He gave Hanuman his ring. `Take this ring,' he said. `When you find Sita, show her this ring. She will then know that you have come from me. I am depending on you to find Sita.'

Thus a fourth division of the army was formed. It was led by Hanuman. Among its members was Angad, the son of Bali, and Jambavan, king of the bears. This group went towards the south because Jatayu had told Ram that Ravan had taken Sita southwards. Each group was keen to prove itself and find out where Sita was.

The divisions that had gone north, west and east returned in a month's time. They reported that Sita was not to be found anywhere. Their leaders said, `We have searched through forests, mountains and cities but could not find Sita. Jatayu told Ram that the rakshas carrying Sita had gone south. Hanuman has gone south and he has not yet returned. It is possible that he has found some clue as to where Sita is.'

Meanwhile Hanuman, Angad, Jambavan and the others had reached the Vindhya mountains. They searched every nook and cranny of the hills and woods. They looked inside caves, but found no sign of Sita. Determined not to give up, they travelled further south. They passed through a vast barren area where the trees had neither fruit nor flowers. The rivers were dry. There were no animals. Even birdsong did not break the deathlike silence.

At last, faint from hunger and thirst, they came upon a cave almost hidden by dense creepers. Usually they never entered a cave without first making sure that there were no rakshasas or wild animals inside.

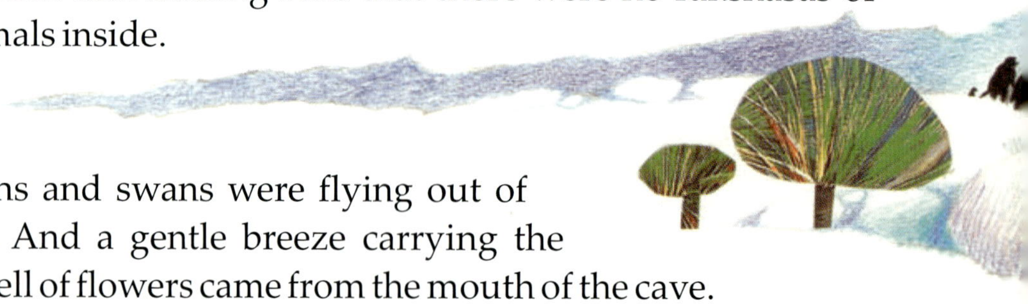

But herons and swans were flying out of the cave. And a gentle breeze carrying the sweet smell of flowers came from the mouth of the cave.

Hanuman said, `There must be a stream inside the cave.' Following Hanuman the monkeys, holding on to each other, slowly entered the cave. Going further they came upon a brightly lit area. They were in a grove of trees. The trees were laden with flowers and fruit and birds sang among the branches. The grove led to a beautiful city. The streets of the city glittered and shone. The houses were made of gold and silver and set with precious stones.

The monkeys saw an old sanyasin seated on a deerskin. At first they were afraid to go near her. But Hanuman plucked up courage and went up to her. He asked her who she was and what was the city with houses made of gold and silver.

The sanyasin told him that the city was a work of magic. It was built by the architect of the demons. She offered the monkeys food and water. Hanuman told her who they were and that they were searching for Sita.

The sanyasin said, `No one who enters this cave can leave it alive. But you are special because you are looking for Sita. So I will use my powers to help you get out of here. Close your eyes.'

The monkeys covered their eyes with their hands. When they opened their eyes, they found themselves on the seashore. At first they were happy. But their happiness soon turned to dismay. It was already spring. The trees had put forth fresh young leaves and the grass was green. It meant that a long time had passed since they had parted from Ram and Sugreev. They had been given a month's time to look for Sita. That month was long over.

Angad was very unhappy. He said, `If we return to Kishkinda without news of Sita, our king Sugreev will surely kill us. It is better that we stay here and fast till we die.'

The others agreed. They all lay down on the ground, prepared to fast unto death. As they lay there, they began to talk of past events. They said, `It is all because of Kaikeyi that we are starving ourselves to death. If she had not demanded that Ram be sent away to the forest, Ravan could not have carried away Sita. The heroic Jatayu even lost his life trying to save Sita!'

When they mentioned Jatayu's name, someone called from a nearby hill. It was Jatayu's elder brother, Sampati, who was known for his courage and strength. He had grown old and his wings had been burnt by the sun. So he could not move, but he was keen to get news of his brother.

Angad told him how Jatayu had met his end. Angad also asked Sampati if he knew where Sita could be.

Sampati replied, `I saw Ravan carrying away a beautiful young woman across the sea to Lanka. She was crying, "O Ram! O Lakshman!" She must have been Sita and she is now a prisoner in Lanka. The city is far, far away in the middle of the ocean.'

The monkeys were overjoyed to get news of Sita. They shouted, `Now we need not think of dying. Our king will be very pleased with us.' Sampati's troubles were also over. Some time earlier, the gods had granted him a boon. He was told that he would get back his wings if he helped Ram. And he had helped Ram by telling the monkeys where Ravan had taken Sita. As a result of the boon, new feathers began to grow on Sampati. Able to fly again, he rose into the sky.

The monkeys sat near the seashore and began to plan their next move. Who could cross the sea and bring news of Sita? Angad asked, `Tell me, O mighty warriors, which is the farthest that you can jump?'

One of the monkeys said, `I can jump quite far, but it will not be enough to take me across the sea.'

Another monkey said that he could jump twice as far. Yet another that he could jump thrice as far, and so on. But the farthest that any of them could manage still fell short of the distance needed to cross the sea.

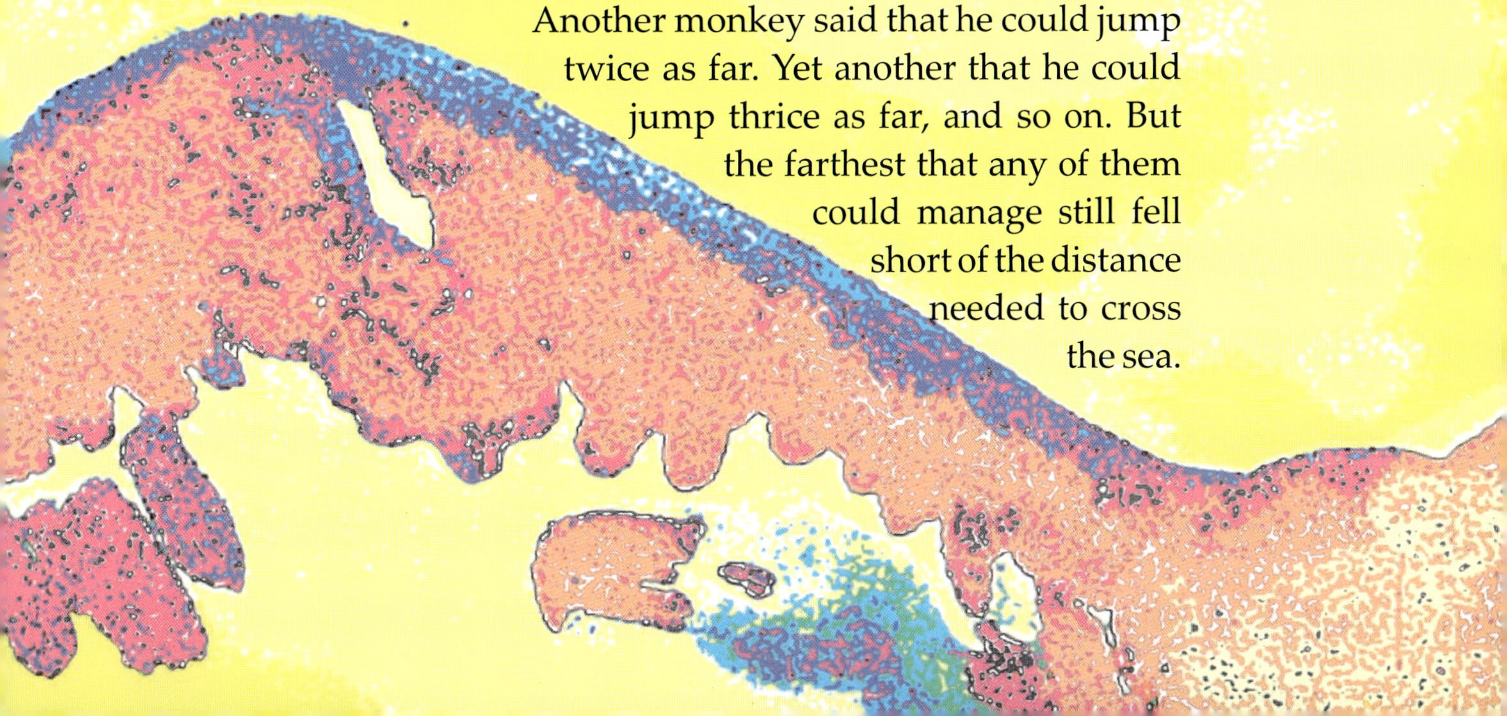

When Angad's turn came he said, `I can certainly jump far enough to reach Lanka on the other side of the ocean. But I will not have the strength to do a second jump that long and return from Lanka.'

The monkeys were very worried. They were very keen to help Ram. They had found out that Sita was a prisoner in Lanka. But none of them could go and meet Sita and bring back news of her.

At this point, Jambavan looked at the great Hanuman. Hanuman was sitting apart from the others, deep in thought. Jambavan asked, `Hanuman, O great warrior, why do you sit apart? Why are you silent? Do you not know your great strength? Crossing the sea will not be difficult for you.'

Hanuman heard Jambavan and was reminded of his great strength. He began to grow in size. His face and body glowed. `I am the son of Vayu, the wind god,' Hanuman said to Jambavan. `I can go anywhere and few can equal me in speed. I shall surely be able to see Sita and return with news of her. But, to take such a long jump, I must climb a hill and press my foot hard against it. The hill should be able to stand the pressure of my foot. It must not crumble under the pressure.'

Hanuman climbed up Mahendra hill. Standing at the top, he offered prayers to the gods. Then he pressed his foot hard against the hill. So

great was the pressure of his foot that sparks flew from the ground and springs of water flowed out from the hill. Trees shook and trembled. Huge serpents hiding among rocks came out of their holes, hissing. Hanuman roared and lashed his tail against the ground. Then, gathering all his strength, he took a mighty leap and flew into the sky with the speed of an arrow. His flight led to a storm that uprooted many trees. These trees followed him part of the way, shedding their flowers in the air. Then they fell into the sea.

Hanuman was determined to reach Lanka and bring back news of Sita. On the way he came across many obstacles. Once, when he was travelling over the sea, he felt himself being pulled down by a great force. He looked down and saw a huge she-demon pulling him down by his shadow. She had opened her mouth to swallow him. Hanuman entered her mouth, tore his way through her body and came out. He was not hurt. But the she-demon died and sank into the sea.

Thus Hanuman fought many dangers with courage as he flew towards Lanka. At last he came to the coast of Lanka. It was covered with banana and coconut trees. Hanuman came to rest on a hilltop and reduced his size to that of an ordinary monkey.

From the hilltop Hanuman gazed in wonder at the grand city of Lanka. Built on top of a mountain, it seemed like the city of the gods. There were majestic buildings, well-planned markets and streets. There were woods and groves, parks and gardens, lakes and ponds. Moats surrounded the city to keep enemies out. Well-armed, terrifying rakshasas with sharp nails and teeth stood on guard, defending the city and those who lived in it. Hanuman wondered aloud, 'Even if Sugreev's army manages to reach Lanka, how can we hope to conquer this great city?' But next minute he checked himself. 'I must first find out if Sita is here. Other things can wait.'

Hanuman climbed over the city wall and jumped into the street below. He walked from street to street. Wherever he went, he heard the sound of music coming from the big houses. Hanuman went from house to house, and carefully looked inside each. He saw many women, but there was no sign of Sita. Hanuman even entered Ravan's palace. It was very early in the morning and Ravan lay asleep. Even in his sleep he looked very powerful. In the palace Hanuman saw many beautiful women wearing the loveliest of clothes and jewellery. They were fast asleep. But Sita was not among them.

Hanuman went from garden to garden, searching for Sita. But there was no sign of her. Finally he said to himself in despair, `Am I to return without seeing Sita? It would be better for me not to go back. I shall end my life here . . . '

Then Hanuman saw the grove, Ashok Vatika. It was a beautiful garden attached to a temple and surrounded by a high wall. Hanuman jumped on to the wall. From there he jumped on to the branch of a tall tree with a dense crown of leaves and looked around.

When he looked down he saw a most beautiful woman sitting under the tree. She was thin and pale and looked very sad. She sighed again and again. `This must be Sita,' thought Hanuman.

Sita was surrounded by fierce-looking, ugly rakshasis, who guarded her night and day. Hanuman was wondering how he could attract Sita's attention, when Ravan entered the garden. He was dressed in spotless white and was surrounded by beautiful maidens. Ravan walked up to Sita. Once again he told her how powerful and rich he was. He spoke ill of Ram. He told Sita to give up thoughts of Ram.

Sita was very angry when she heard Ravan's

words. She said, `Your wealth and power do not tempt me. I warn you: if you continue on this sinful path, you will soon meet your end.' And Sita turned her back on Ravan.

Ravan was furious. `Very well, then,' he said. `Only two months remain of the twelve that I had given you. If at the end of two months you still do not agree to marry me, you shall be cut to pieces.'

With these words Ravan left. The rakshasis gathered around Sita and began to threaten her. `Give up Ram and take Ravan as your husband,' they said, `or we shall kill you and make a meal of you.' Sita began to cry. She had nobody to comfort her. But one old rakshasi said, `Do not trouble this saintly woman. Beg her forgiveness. I fear bad times lie ahead for Lanka. Just before dawn I had a dream. I dreamt that Ram came to Lanka. He shone like the sun and carried away Sita on an elephant. I saw Ravan dressed in black, with a garland of red flowers around his neck. He was riding a chariot drawn by donkeys . . . I saw Lanka plunge into the sea.'

Hidden by the leaves around him, Hanuman heard everything. He had seen Ravan's city. He knew the weak spots in its defences. He had also seen Sita. He knew that she was alive. But he was worried about her. He thought, `She looks so unhappy. I must talk to her and give her courage. Otherwise she may kill herself.'

Hanuman did not wish to frighten Sita. He thought, `If I appear before her suddenly, she will get frightened. She will think it is one of Ravan's tricks. I must be very careful.'

With this in mind, he began to relate the story of Ram's life. He related the story in a sweet and gentle voice. Sita heard him and was filled with wonder. She looked around. There was no one there except a little monkey sitting in the tree overhead. `Am I dreaming?' said Sita to herself. `Or is it possible that this is really a messenger from my Ram?'

At this thought, Sita's face lit up with happiness. Hanuman chose that moment to come down and speak to her. He gave her Ram's ring. When she saw the ring, Sita was sure that the little monkey really was Ram's messenger. Hanuman told her all that had happened since she was carried away. He said, `Ram, Lakshman, Sugreev and the entire army of mighty monkeys and bears will soon be here. Ram will kill Ravan and rescue you. He will destroy Lanka with all its rakshasas. Do not lose heart.'

Then Hanuman had an idea. He said to Sita, 'Why should you wait till Lanka is destroyed? Why should you suffer any longer? I can carry you across the ocean on my back and take you to Ram right away.'

But Sita replied, 'When the rakshasas see you carry me away they will attack you. How will you fight them and protect me at the same time? Besides, if you carry me away quietly, what will people think of Ram? They will think he is a coward, without the courage to fight Ravan. Let Ram come like a true warrior, destroy Lanka and take me back.'

Sita gave Hanuman a jewel that she wore in her hair. She said, `Give this to my Ram and he will know that you have really met me.' Hanuman bowed, accepted the jewel and took leave of Sita.

After taking leave of Sita, Hanuman sat for a while on the garden wall. He wondered, `What can I do to give Sita courage and fill Ravan with fear?' Finally he decided to make a show of his strength.

Hanuman began to grow in size. Soon he became huge. Then he began to destroy the garden. He pulled out trees, plants and creepers by their roots. The beautiful Ashok Vatika became a ruin. The deer and birds that lived there fled in panic. The only tree that Hanuman spared was the one under which Sita was sitting.

The rakshasis guarding Sita were terrified. They ran to tell Ravan what had happened. Ravan was furious and sent a strong force to kill the monkey. But Hanuman attacked them fiercely. Roaring `Long live Ram. The end of Lanka is near,' he killed them all.

Hanuman' s roar rang through Lanka and filled the rakshasas with terror. When Ravan heard that his warriors had been killed, his eyes blazed with anger. He sent five great generals at the head of a huge army to kill the monkey. But it was not easy to overpower Hanuman. He attacked them with huge rocks and trees. He killed all the generals, along with their soldiers.

Next Ravan sent his son Indrajit. Indrajit shot one arrow after another at Hanuman. Hanuman rose in the sky and struck the

arrows down. He uprooted a big tree and knocked Indrajit off his chariot. He caught the demons who had come with Indrajit, and crushed them one by one.

Finally Indrajit shot the Brahmastra at Hanuman. This was a divine weapon which Indrajit had received from Lord Brahma. The moment the Brahmastra touched Hanuman's body he fell down, completely helpless.

When the rakshasas saw Hanuman helpless and lying on the ground, they tied him up with ropes. They did not know that when ropes were used for tying up a victim, the Brahmastra lost its powers. Hanuman knew this, but still pretended to be helpless.

Indrajit ordered that Hanuman be taken to Ravan's court. `Let my father decide what is to be done with this monkey who is bent on destroying Lanka.'

Hanuman welcomed this chance of meeting Ravan face to face. He allowed himself to be dragged through the streets of Lanka. He remained quiet when

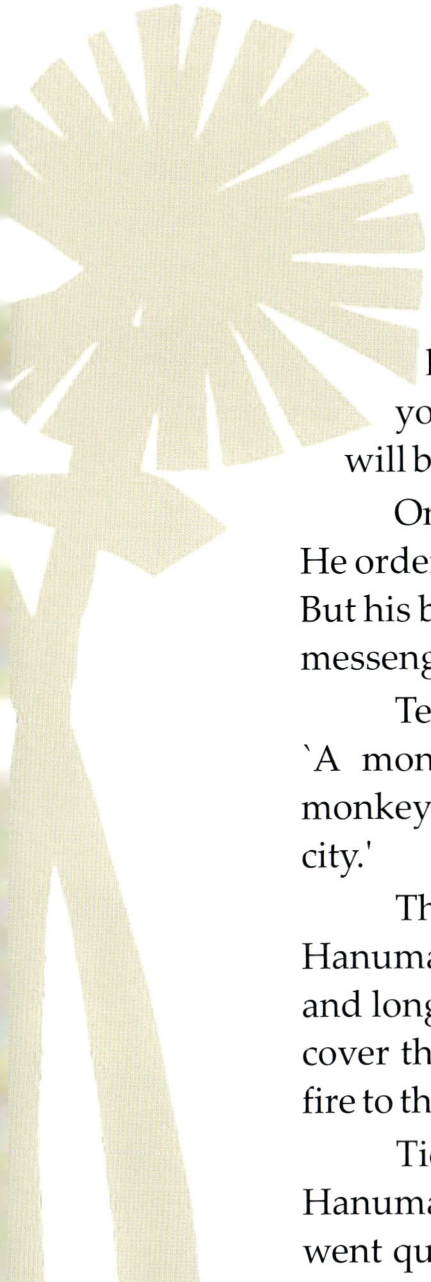

the people of Lanka kicked and beat him and made fun of him. But when he was brought before Ravan, he spoke boldly. He said to Ravan, `It was not right to carry off Sita. Return her to Ram. Do not make Ram your enemy or you and all the rakshasas will be killed and Lanka will be destroyed.'

On hearing this, Ravan's eyes blazed with anger. He ordered that Hanuman be put to death immediately. But his brother Vibheeshan said, `He has come here as a messenger. It is not right to put a messenger to death.'

Ten-headed Ravan listened to this advice. He said, `A monkey greatly values his tail. Set fire to the monkey's tail and take him through the streets of the city.'

The rakshasas wrapped cotton rags around Hanuman's tail. But as they did so, the tail grew longer and longer. So they had to bring more and more rags to cover the tail. Then they soaked the rags in oil and set fire to them.

Tied up with ropes and with his tail on fire, Hanuman was taken through the streets of Lanka. He went quietly, carefully observing the secrets of the city and its defences. He was thinking, `What miracle is this? The fire burns brightly on my tail yet it does not hurt me. This must be because of Sita's blessings.'

Suddenly Hanuman shrank in size. The ropes that bound him became loose. He shook them off. He was free.

Once again Hanuman grew and grew till he was an enormous size. In one great bound he jumped on to the top of a tall building. He swung his tail and set fire to the building. Jumping from one rooftop to another, he set fire to many houses. A strong wind made the fire burn more fiercely. Soon it had spread all over the city. Palaces, towers and mansions were burnt to ashes.

Hanuman sat on top of a hill and watched the city burn. Finally he jumped into the sea and put out the fire on his tail.

Before leaving Lanka, Hanuman again shrank in size and went to meet Sita. Bowing low before her he said, 'I promise you, Ram and Lakshman will soon be here to set you free. Take courage.'

Sita blessed him as he took leave of her. Then Hanuman climbed to the top of a hill and leapt into the sky. Flying at the speed of an arrow, he crossed the ocean. When he saw Mahendra hill, he roared with happiness. Far below, on the ground, the monkeys heard him. They jumped about for joy. They said, 'Hanuman

must have brought good news about Sita or he would not have roared like that.'

As soon as Hanuman landed on Mahendra hill, the monkeys surrounded him. They were eager to get news of Sita and to hear about Ravan and his kingdom. Hanuman told them everything. Then he asked, `Shall we go to Lanka right away? We can kill Ravan and bring Sita back.'

Many of the monkeys wanted to leave for Lanka right away. Angad, in particular, was keen to go into battle against Ravan. But Jambavan advised them not to be so hasty. `Let us go to Kishkinda. Ram and Lakshman must be waiting for us. Let us find out what they wish to do.'

The others accepted his advice. The entire army returned to Kishkinda.

They met Ram, Lakshman and Sugreev. Hanuman told them how he had met Sita. He also showed Ram the jewel that Sita had given him. When he saw the jewel, Ram was overcome by grief. He was grateful to Hanuman for all that he had done. He embraced Hanuman and said, `You have done what nobody else could do. You are a true friend.'

It was decided that the monkey army should go to Lanka, fight, kill Ravan and bring Sita back. So Ram, Lakshman and Sugreev set out for Lanka, followed by the army of monkeys and bears. They lived on honey and fruit. As they marched, many trees were uprooted and flowering creepers were crushed under their feet.

When they reached the seashore, Ram said, `A vast ocean lies between us and Lanka. How is the army going to cross the ocean?'

Nobody had an answer to this question. `Till we can think of a way to cross the ocean, let the army camp in the forest,' said Ram.

Sugreev passed on the orders to the commanders. The commanders told the soldiers. Before long the army had set up camp in the forest and along the seashore. They looked at the endless waters filled with fish, sea monsters and serpents and wondered how they would cross the vast ocean.

As we have seen, Hanuman set fire to Lanka and flew back to Mahendra hill. In Lanka, Ravan was shocked at what Hanuman had done to his city. He called a meeting of his ministers and advisers. He said, `What happened today has never happened before. Ram's messenger not only managed to enter Lanka, which is heavily guarded, he even met Sita and talked to her.

He destroyed houses and palaces and killed some of our bravest warriors. Ram is a bitter enemy of the rakshasas. He will soon be here with his army of millions of monkeys and bears. I have called this meeting to decide how we should deal with this enemy.'

One by one the rakshas warriors promised their support to Ravan. They praised Ravan's powers. Each boasted that he would kill Ram, Lakshman and Sugreev. They also said they would kill Hanuman who had caused so much trouble in Lanka. Ravan's warriors were not being simply boastful. They had no idea of the strength of Ram, Lakshman and the army of mighty monkeys. They were also trying to please their king. And Ravan was pleased.

But Vibheeshan, younger brother of Ravan, disagreed. With folded hands he said, `Brother, what your warriors have said may be pleasing to the ear, but it is not true. The enemy have a very large and powerful army. Your advisers are not giving you good advice. It was wrong of you to carry away Sita. Ram killed the rakshasas at Panchvati in order to defend himself. Who can blame him for that? Return Sita to Ram. Do what is right. Otherwise this lovely city of Lanka will be destroyed and all these brave rakshasas will be killed.'

When he heard this, Ravan flew into a rage. Accusing his brother of being disloyal, he said, 'If anybody else had spoken these words, Vibheeshan, I would have killed him. You are a disgrace to our family!'

The next day, Ravan again called a meeting of his ministers and advisers. He said, 'I have thought it over. I shall not give up Sita. Ram and Lakshman are camping by the sea, along with the monkey army. It will be very difficult for them to cross over to Lanka. But even if they succeed in doing so, we must not be afraid of them. We must think how we can kill those two.'

Besides Vibheeshan, Ravan had another younger brother, Kumbhkaran. He used to sleep for months at a time. Once asleep, it was almost impossible to wake him up. But at this time he was awake. He now spoke fearlessly before Ravan, 'Great king, you should have met Ram face to face and killed him before carrying off Sita. What you did was very wrong.'

At these words Ravan looked very unhappy. Kumbhkaran loved his brother and did not wish to make him unhappy. He said, `Brother, what you did may have been wrong, but I am with you. Do not worry. I shall kill Ram. Just think of ways of killing Lakshman and the monkey warriors.'

A few other rakshas chiefs also spoke in support of Ravan. Only Vibheeshan did not. He said, `Listen to me, my brother. Keeping Sita here will mean certain death for all of us. I beg of you, return her to Ram.'

Ravan flew into a terrible rage. He shouted, `I shall take no more of this from you. Get out of my sight.'

Vibheeshan could not bear this insult. He said, `Very well, my brother. I have tried to warn you, but you will not listen. You can do as you like. I am leaving.'

With that Vibheeshan rose in the air and went straight to Ram's camp on the other side of the ocean. Four of his rakshas friends went with him.

Sugreev and the monkeys on the ground saw Vibheeshan coming through the air. Sugreev said to Hanuman, `This rakshas has surely come along with his companions to spy on us.' And the monkeys armed themselves with rocks and trees to kill Vibheeshan and his companions.

When Vibheeshan reached there, he said, `I am Vibheeshan, younger brother of Ravan. I tried to reason with Ravan and told him to return Sita to Ram. But he would not listen to me. He has

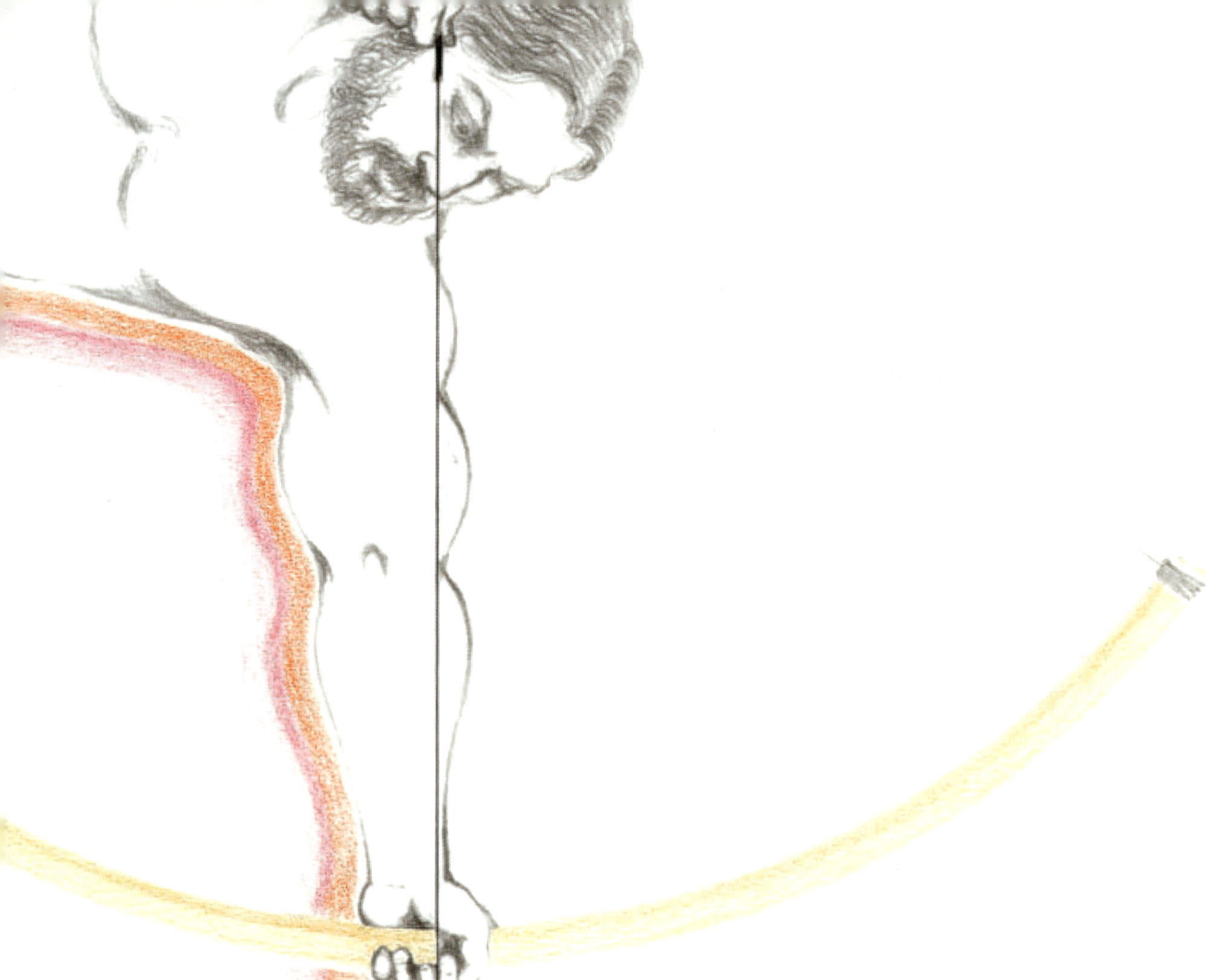

insulted me. I have come to join Ram.'

Sugreev still did not trust Vibheeshan. He thought Vibheeshan was trying to trick them and had been sent by Ravan as a spy. But Hanuman said, `Vibheeshan does not seem to be telling a lie. His face is open and friendly.'

Ram said, `Vibheeshan has come to me looking for shelter. I cannot turn him away. I accept him as an ally.'

Lakshman and Sugreev took a little water from the sea, sprinkled a few drops over Vibheeshan and declared him king of Lanka. Vibheeshan said, `I will do my best to help you conquer Lanka and get back Sita.'

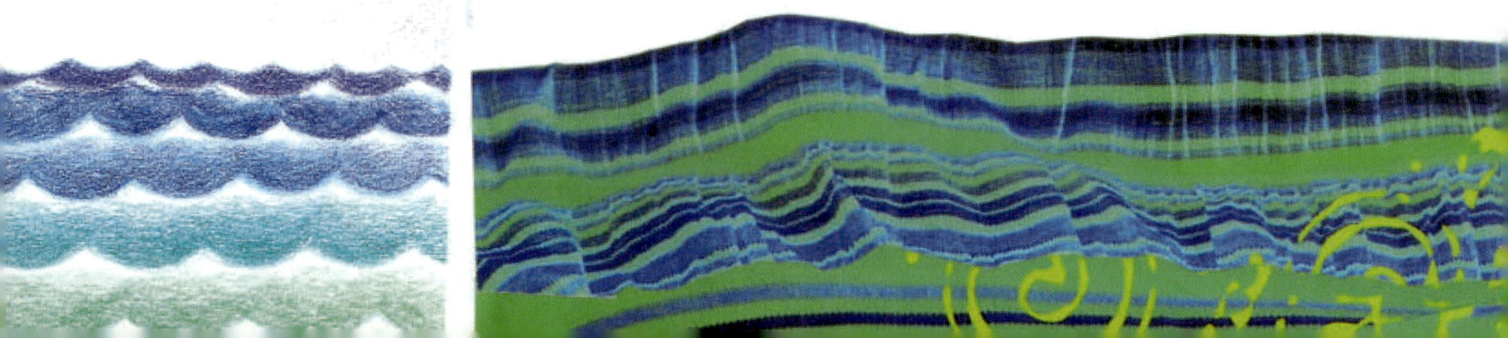

Ram asked, `How will we cross the ocean? It is full of crocodiles, sea serpents and fish. It is also very deep.'

Sugreev and Vibheeshan began to discuss how they should cross the ocean. Vibheeshan suggested that Ram ask the ocean for help. The others agreed.

So Ram spread some holy grass on the seashore and sat down on it. For three days and three nights he prayed to the god of the ocean. He asked the god to grant him a passage to the other side. But the god of the ocean did not appear before him. Ram became angry. He said, `The god of the ocean has become very proud. I shall teach him a lesson. Bring me my bow and arrows, Lakshman.'

Ram took his mighty bow and shot arrows like thunderbolts into the ocean. With the force of the arrows the earth trembled and waves as high as mountains rose from the ocean. Fish and sea serpents crashed to the shore in thousands. Then the god of the ocean rose from the waters. He stood before Ram with folded hands and said, `My lord, it is my nature to be vast and deep. I cannot let anyone walk across my surface. But this much I can do: ask the monkeys to bring rocks and trees and build a bridge over my surface. I shall keep the rocks and trees in place. My waves will not wash them away. You can cross over this bridge to Lanka. May victory be yours!'

This seemed a good plan. Thousands of monkeys ran and uprooted trees to make the bridge. They broke off mountain peaks and rolled down huge rocks to the shore. They laid these out on the waters of the ocean. Finally they covered these with grass and small pieces of wood to make a smooth path to walk on. There was so much noise that nobody could hear the roar of the ocean.

Ram's heart filled with joy to see the army of monkeys and bears work so willingly to build the bridge. How keen they were to help Ram and bring Sita back from Lanka! But somebody else was also keen to help Ram. And that somebody was much smaller than the monkeys and bears. Let me tell you about her.

One day, while the work on the bridge was going on, a small brown squirrel came running to the shore. She had a small pebble in her mouth. She put the pebble near a big rock. Then she ran back for more pebbles. Back and forth, back and forth ran the squirrel.

Some of the monkeys noticed what the squirrel was doing. They laughed. `Look at her,' they said. `She really thinks she is helping us! Imagine bringing little pebbles to build a big bridge like this!' The bears, too laughed. One of them even tried to catch the squirrel. But she was too quick for him.

Dodging the bears and monkeys, the little squirrel ran to Ram. He was talking to someone and did not notice her. The squirrel stood up on two legs and said as loud as she could, `Those horrid bears and monkeys are making fun of me. Tell them to stop. I also want to help build the bridge so you can cross over to Lanka and bring back Sita Ma.'

Ram heard the tiny voice of the squirrel above the roar of the ocean and the noise of bridge building. He bent down and lifted up the squirrel in his hands. His heart melted to see that she had tears in her eyes. `Little one,' said Ram, `I am very grateful for your help. The bridge will be stronger because of the pebbles brought by you. Nobody will make fun of you again.' And Ram gently stroked the squirrel's back with his fingers. When he raised his hand, the marks of his fingers shone white against the dark fur of the squirrel. Ever since then the squirrel has had these three white stripes on her back. They are a token of Ram's love for her.

The god of the ocean was true to his word. He kept the trees and boulders in place. Soon the great bridge was ready. Thousands of monkeys and bears crossed the bridge into Lanka. So great was the crowd on the bridge that some of the monkeys flew through the air, others climbed on crocodiles, fish and serpents and crossed over to the other side.

That night the army of monkeys and bears rested on a hill overlooking Ravan's city. The following morning they stood on top of the hill and took a good look at the city. It was built on a hill and was very beautiful. The fortress inside the city was huge. Its walls were thick and its gates were heavily guarded. It did not seem possible to conquer it. The rakshas army guarded the fortress. It was such a large army, it looked like a second wall surrounding the fortress.

Ram decided on a plan of attack. The army entered the forest surrounding the city. They split into four divisions, so as to attack the fortress from four different directions – north, south, east and west. Each division had its own leader.

Ram made one last effort to avoid war. He sent for Angad and said, `Go to Ravan and give him a message from me.'

Angad rose in the air and soon stood before Ravan. He introduced himself and said, `I come as Ram's messenger. The end of your sinful life is near. If you want to live, return Sita to Ram and beg him to forgive you. You cannot hope to win against Ram.'

Ravan lost his temper. He shouted, `Catch him! Kill him.' At once four rakshasas caught hold of Angad. But he rose into the sky, carrying the rakshasas with him. From a great height he dashed them to the ground. Then, with a single kick, he broke the tower of the palace, and returned to the army of monkeys.

Ravan and the rakshasas were filled with fear at this show of strength. But they tried to hide their fear. Ravan made one last attempt to win over Sita. He thought, `If Sita agrees to be my wife, Ram will be filled with shame. He will be heartbroken and will go away from Lanka.' Ravan sent for a magician. `Make a head that looks just like Ram's. Bring it to Ashok Vatika,' he said.

Ravan then went to Ashok Vatika and tried to win over Sita. He said, `Why do you still think of Ram? He and his army have been destroyed. My warriors attacked them while they were asleep. Now agree to be my wife. Be the queen of Lanka.'

Just then the magician entered Ashok Vatika with the false head of Ram. Sita saw the head and began to cry. As Sita was crying, Ravan's ministers and generals sent word that they wanted to see him immediately. The moment Ravan left Ashok Vatika, the magic spell broke. The false head of Ram disappeared.

One of the rakshasis guarding Sita tried to comfort her. `Ram has not been killed,' she said. `He has reached Lanka at the head of a large army and is getting ready to attack.' Just then Sita heard the beating of drums and the blaring of conch shells. Sita was very happy. The rakshasas heard the same sounds and trembled with fear.

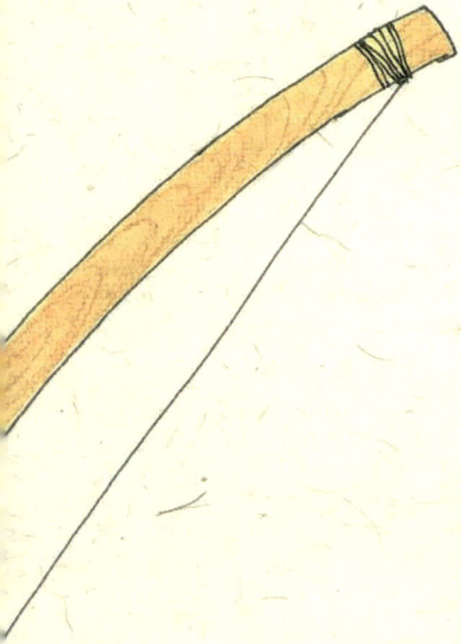

Ram gave orders to the army to attack. They began to hurl huge rocks and trees at the city walls and gates. The rakshasas came out and fell upon the monkeys with spears and clubs. In reply the monkeys fought the rakshasas with their teeth and nails, with trees that they uprooted and with rocks. This terrible battle between the monkeys and bears and the rakshasas went on all day. It went on all night as well. Thousands of rakshasas were killed and so were thousands of monkeys.

Riding his chariot, Ravan's son Indrajit joined the battle. Angad attacked him and destroyed his chariot. Indrajit rose into the air and made himself invisible. Then he shot arrow after arrow at Ram and Lakshman.

These were not really arrows. They were poisonous snakes which had become arrows through Indrajit's magic. The snakes coiled themselves around Ram and Lakshman and the two princes could not move. They fell on to the battlefield, helpless. They could not even open their eyes. When the monkeys saw this, they were filled with fear and began to run away.

But help was on its way, and from a very powerful friend. That friend was Garuda, the eagle king of the birds. He was the mount of Lord Vishnu. And Ram was none other than Lord Vishnu in human form. Garuda had seen that Ram was in trouble, so he rushed to help.

As Garuda flew over the battlefield, his powerful wings raised a mighty wind. The poisonous snakes saw him and fled. The eagle is an enemy of snakes. He kills and eats them.

When the snakes had disappeared, Garuda came and sat near Ram and Lakshman. With his beak he gently stroked the princes' wounds. Soon Ram and Lakshman had recovered completely. Seeing this, the monkeys came back. Once again they began to attack Ravan's fortress. They shouted and beat their drums as they did so.

Ravan was inside the fortress when he heard the joyful shouts of the monkeys. He sent some rakshasas to find out what had happened. When they returned they said, `Ram and Lakshman have shaken off the snakes. They are again ready for battle. Their army is attacking the fortress with even greater force than before.'

Ravan's heart sank. `Till now nobody has escaped those snakes,' he said. `If Ram and Lakshman were able to free themselves, they must really be very strong. Lanka is in real danger.'

Ravan now mounted his chariot and came to the battlefield. He killed hundreds of monkeys and bears.

Ravan shot many arrows at Lakshman, but Lakshman blocked them with his shield. Finally Ravan hurled a spear at Lakshman. It hit Lakshman in the chest, and he fell to the ground.

Ram saw this and decided to go after Ravan. But he did not have a chariot. Riding on Hanuman's shoulders, Ram attacked Ravan and wounded him. Ravan's bow fell from his hand. His chariot was smashed and his golden crown broke into pieces. Ravan stood before Ram, unarmed and helpless. But Ram did not attack him. He said, `You have fought very hard today and need to rest. Go back to your fortress. Come back tomorrow with fresh weapons.'

Ravan went back to his fortress. But he was ashamed and very unhappy. Later he recovered some of his courage. He ordered his attendants to wake up his brother Kumbhkaran, who usually slept for six months at a time.

It was only nine days since Kumbhkaran had gone to sleep. `Waking him up will be very difficult,' Ravan said to his attendants. `But you must do it. If Kumbhkaran goes to battle, the enemy will surely be destroyed.'

The attendants went to Kumbhkaran's palace. They entered his bed-chamber and saw that he was fast asleep. But even in his sleep, he was frightening. He was huge, his hair stood straight up like a forest and his mouth was wide open. When he breathed out, the blast of wind was so strong that the rakshasas found it difficult to remain on their feet.

The attendants knew that Kumbhkaran would be very, very hungry when he woke up. So they had taken mountains of food for him. They put the food and jars of delicious drinks on both sides of his bed. Then they tried to wake him up. They beat drums and blew conches as loud as they could. They shouted and screamed in his ears. They pushed and shook the huge body. They even made horses and camels walk on him. The city of Lanka rang with the noise they made, but it had no effect on Kumbhkaran. Finally the attendants drove one thousand elephants over Kumbhkaran's body. At last Kumbhkaran opened his eyes.

With one sweep of his arms Kumbhkaran brushed aside all the attendants. Then he yawned and began to eat. The mountains of food around him began to disappear. When Kumbhkaran's hunger was somewhat satisfied, he asked, `Why have you woken me up? Is my brother in danger?'

The rakshasas told him what had happened. Kumbhkaran was furious. `I shall go right now and defeat the enemy,' he roared. `And I shall kill Ram and Lakshman.'

The attendants were very happy to hear this. `But first meet the king,' they said to Kumbhkaran.

Ravan was delighted to see Kumbhkaran. He said, `Ram, son of Dasharath, is destroying us. Thousands of monkeys and bears are helping him. They have built a bridge across the ocean and have surrounded Lanka. Our warriors who went to fight them have been killed.

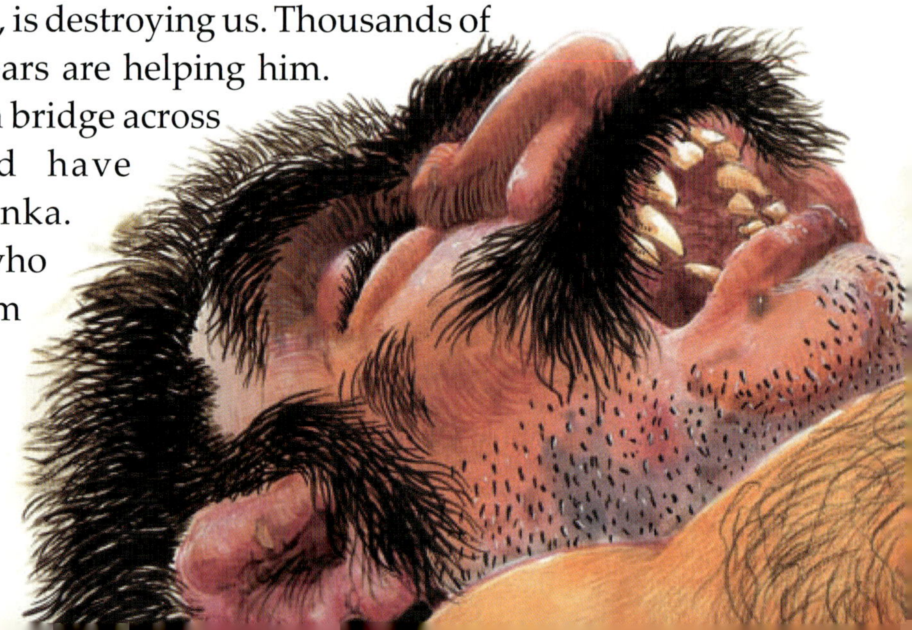

Only you can save the rakshasas. Help me, my brother. Go at once. Destroy our enemy and save Lanka.'

Once again Kumbhkaran told Ravan, 'I wish you had not carried off Sita. It is that act of yours which has brought all this

trouble on us. But I am your brother. I will always stand by you. I shall destroy the monkey army and bring back, as a gift for you, the head of Ram.' Kumbhkaran embraced his brother and, armed with a spear, marched into battle. Behind him marched a large army of rakshasas.

Kumbhkaran was really huge. The earth shook when he walked. At the sight of him, the monkeys began to run helter skelter. They had only rocks and trees to fight with. And Kumbhkaran brushed these aside like drops of rain. He killed hundreds of bears and monkeys. Others ran away and tried to hide in the forest. Lakshman tried to stop Kumbhkaran, but the rakshas took no notice of him. He rushed to attack Ram.

Ram faced Kumbhkaran. He picked up his mighty bow and shot several arrows at Kumbhkaran. But these had no effect. Then Ram shot sharper and more powerful arrows. These cut off Kumbhkaran's legs. But the rakshas kept moving forward and fighting furiously. Finally Ram took careful aim and, with a powerful arrow, cut off Kumbhkaran's head.

When Ravan heard the news he was stunned. 'What use is my kingdom to me now that my brother, the mighty Kumbhkaran is dead?' he cried.

Ravan ordered that the defences of the fortress be repaired. Then he went back to his palace. He was very unhappy.

Seeing his father looking unhappy, Indrajit said, `Father, why are you so upset? I shall defeat your enemy. Before the day ends, Ram and Lakshman will be dead, killed by my arrows.'

Indrajit mounted his chariot and came out of the fortress at the head of a large army. They were heavily armed. Indrajit led them to the battlefield. Once again he made himself invisible and rose into the sky. He began to shower arrows on the monkey army. The monkeys lost hundreds of their warriors. But they did not lose heart. They fought back. But how could they fight an enemy whom they could not see?

Indrajit then turned on Ram and Lakshman. He shot arrows at them, bright as the rays of the sun, but these had no effect on Ram and Lakshman. Finally Indrajit discharged the Brahmastra. At this the entire monkey army, along with Ram and Lakshman, became unconscious and fell down on the battlefield.

Vibheeshan and Hanuman saw this. They ran to the battlefield and began to search among the fallen monkeys and bears. They were looking for Jambavan, the king of the bears. Jambavan was old, but he was a great and wise leader.

Finally Hanuman and Vibheeshan found Jambavan. They called out to him and he answered. `I feel so faint that I cannot see

you clearly,' he said. `I can only recognise you by your voices. Hanuman, my son, only you can save Ram, Lakshman and our army. Go at once to Mount Kailash in the Himalayas. There you will find four kinds of herbs which glow in the dark. Bring these back with you. Return before sunrise.'

Hanuman immediately leapt into the sky. He flew over mountains and forests, lakes, rivers and cities till he reached the Himalayas. He came down on Mount Kailash and began to look for the herbs. When the herbs found that someone was looking for them, they made themselves invisible. This made Hanuman angry. He gave the mountain a mighty push. The peak broke off. Hanuman then lifted the peak on his shoulders, along with all the trees and animals, and flew with it south to Lanka and the battlefield. He was back before sunrise.

The smell of the herbs was like a powerful medicine. It immediately revived Ram, Lakshman, and all the monkeys and bears who had fainted. Their wounds also healed. Hanuman then carried the mountain peak back to its place in the Himalayas and returned to Lanka.

When Ram, Lakshman and their army fainted, the battle came to a stop. Indrajit went back to the fortress. But when they revived, the battle started again.

Sugreev ordered some of the monkeys and bears to enter the city and set fire to it. Carrying flaming torches, they burnt down houses and palaces. When Indrajit saw this, he rushed out in his chariot. Once again he used magic against the enemy. This time he created an image of Sita. Grabbing the image by the hair, he dragged it before the monkeys and bears and made a show of killing it. Then he hurled the image down as if it were dead. When the monkeys and bears saw this, they were horrified. The news reached Ram and he could not bear the shock. He sank to the ground.

But Vibheeshan said, `Ravan will never allow Sita to be killed. What Indrajit destroyed was only an image. The truth is, Indrajit has lost all hope of defeating you in battle. Now he wants to make himself so strong that nobody can defeat him. So he is performing a special sacrifice. If he completes the sacrifice, you will not be able to defeat him. Send Lakshman immediately to prevent Indrajit from completing this special sacrifice.'

Ram sent Lakshman, Vibheeshan, Hanuman and many other warriors to Indrajit's palace. Indrajit was busy performing the special sacrifice. Before he could complete the sacrifice, Lakshman attacked him fiercely.

Indrajit mounted his chariot and began to rain arrows on Lakshman. Since Indrajit was riding a chariot, he was at an advantage. Lakshman had no chariot. He mounted Hanuman's shoulders and returned the attack. It was a fierce fight and it went on for hours.

Finally Lakshman used his most powerful weapon, the Indra-astra, given to him by Lord Indra. Uttering the name of Ram, Lakshman shot the weapon. The weapon went hissing through the air and Indrajit's head was cut off from his body.

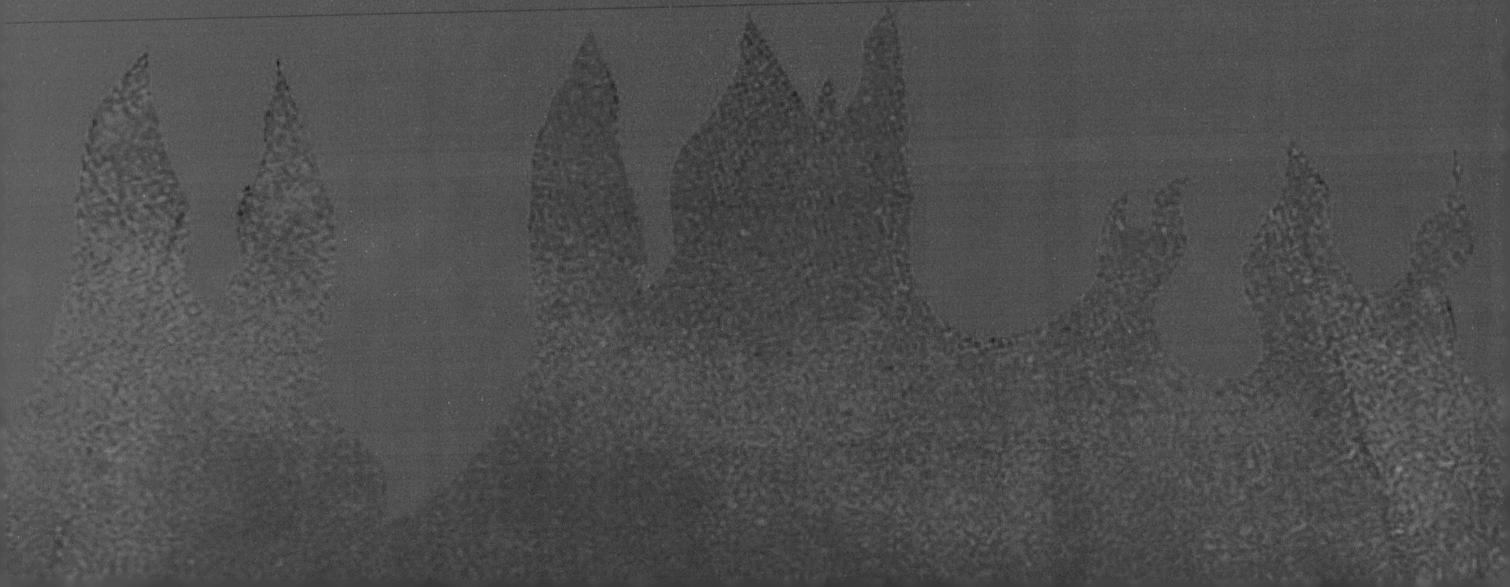

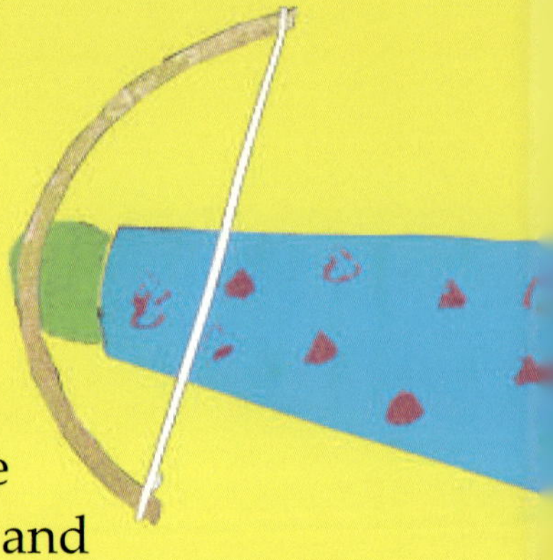

When he heard of Indrajit's fall, Ravan was completely shattered. But he decided to put up one final fight. Most of his generals were dead. He ordered the ones that remained to prepare for battle. Then he mounted his grand chariot drawn by eight horses and came to the battlefield.

Lakshman tried to stop Ravan's advance. But Ravan brushed him aside, forced his way through the army of monkeys and came face to face with Ram. Ravan immediately released a shower of arrows at Ram. Ram blocked them with his own arrows. For a long time these two mighty warriors fought with all the weapons at their command. Each was bent on killing the other.

Ravan was riding his chariot and Ram was fighting from the ground. Ram was at a disadvantage. So Indra, king of the gods, told his charioteer to take his golden chariot for Ram. Ram bowed to the gods in heaven and climbed into the chariot. The grim battle continued.

One after the other, Ram cut off Ravan's ten heads with his arrows. But no sooner was one cut off than another grew in its place. Ram was worried. How would he kill Ravan? Then his charioteer whispered in Ram's ear, `The time for Ravan's destruction has come. Use Brahma's weapon, the Brahmastra, against Ravan.'

Ram immediately took up the Brahmastra. He fitted it to his bow and discharged it with great force. The Brahmastra flew through the air, giving out flames. It struck Ravan in the chest and shattered it. This was the end of Ravan, the demon king of Lanka.

With the fall of Ravan, the battle ended. Vibheeshan was crowned king of Lanka. After the crowning, Ram said to Hanuman, `With King Vibheeshan's permission, enter Lanka. Tell Sita what has happened.'

With Vibheeshan's permission Hanuman went to Ashok Vatika. Sita was overjoyed to get the news of Ram's victory and Ravan's death. She said to Hanuman, `It is because of you that I have lived to see this day. Tell my lord Ram that I am eager to be with him again.'

Vibheeshan came to see Sita and, with folded hands, said, `The monkeys, bears and remaining rakshasas are eager for your darshan. You are a queen. It is only right that they should see you as a queen. I have ordered the palace maidens to attend on you.'

Sita bathed with scented water and the maidens dressed her in silken clothes and glittering jewels. Sita then got into a palanquin and made her way to the army camp.

As soon as they saw the palanquin, the monkeys, bears and rakshasas rushed forward to get a glimpse of the queen for whose sake thousands had died. Ram said, `Tell Sita that she should get down from the palanquin and come to me walking. That way everyone will be able to see her.'

Overjoyed at seeing Ram after such a long time, Sita stepped down from the palanquin and walked up to Ram. But Ram said, `I have killed my enemy and rescued you. I have done my duty. But since you have lived for a year in a stranger's house, I have to assure the people that you are pure.'

On hearing these cruel words Sita's eyes flashed. `How could you say this to me?' she cried. `Is it my fault that the wicked Ravan took me away by force and imprisoned me? But since you doubt me, there is only one thing for me to do.' Weeping, Sita turned to Lakshman. `Brother Lakshman,' she said, `light a fire.'

Lakshman's eyes filled with pain. But he knew that Ram would not change his mind and take Sita back without a trial by fire.

So Lakshman lit a fire.

Her eyes fixed on the ground, Sita went around Ram. Then she bowed to the gods and offered a prayer to Agni, the god of fire. `O Agni, if I am pure, protect me,' she said. With these words Sita walked into the flames.

And do you know what happened? The gods themselves came down from heaven. Brahma said to Ram, `You took human form to rid the world of Ravan. Do you not recognise Sita? She is your own Lakshmi. Take her back. Her place is by your side.'

Sita stood at the heart of the fire. But her body and clothes were not burnt by the flames. Agni lifted her up and brought her to Ram. Ram said, `I knew Sita was pure. But I wanted to assure the people about it. Without this trial by fire, people might have had doubts about her.' And Ram drew Sita to his side.

Ram then asked Indra, `King of the gods, grant that all the monkeys and bears who fought so bravely for my sake and died be brought back to life.'

Indra agreed. The monkeys and bears who had died in battle rose as though waking from a deep sleep. Their wounds were also healed. Indra added, `They will have fresh water, roots and fruits to eat all through the year.' The gods then returned to heaven.

Ram, Lakshman and Sita got into the magical chariot, Pushpak. It carried them swiftly through the air towards Ayodhya. With them in the chariot were Vibheeshan and their monkey and bear friends who wanted to go to Ayodhya to see Ram crowned king.

The chariot alighted at the ashram of Sage Bhardwaj. Bharat was living in a village near the ashram. Ram sent Hanuman ahead to give Bharat news of their arrival. Bharat was overjoyed. He embraced Hanuman and said, `I beg you, take me to Ram.' Bharat, Shatrughan, and the three queen mothers set off for the ashram. Out of respect for Ram, Bharat carried Ram's sandals on his head.

When they reached the ashram Bharat ran and fell at Ram's feet. The two brothers embraced. Bharat put the sandals on Ram's feet. The people who had gone with Bharat began to beat drums and blow conches to show their joy.

All of them then returned to Ayodhya. The city was

decorated with flowers and the streets sprinkled with rose water. Music filled the air to welcome them. Ram was crowned king, as his father had desired.

With Ram as king, there was happiness everywhere. There was no more sorrow, and no more sickness. Nobody was poor. Nobody wished to harm another. The rains were plentiful. Crops grew well and the rivers flowed with clean, pure water. The trees in the forest always bore flowers and fruit. Birds sang and animals wandered around without fear. Man and beast were happy when Ram was king.